ALSO BY JUNE J. MCINERNEY

FICTION
The Prisoner's Portrait
Forty-Thirty
Rainbow in the Sky
Cats of Nine Tales
The Basset Chronicles
Adventures of Oreigh Ogglefont

NON-FICTION
Meditations for New Members

POETRY COLLECTIONS
Spinach Water
Exodus Ending

MUSICALS
We Three Kings
Noah's Rainbow
Beauty and the Beast
Peter, the Wolf, and Red Riding Hood

the
Schuylkill
Monster

A Novel of Phoenixville in 1978

June J. McInerney

Don't believe everything
that you read in the newspapers.
ANDREW CARD

PROLOGUE

Located at 40°7'51"N 75°31'9"W, Phoenixville was settled in 1732 and was originally called Manavon. In 1790, the French Creek Nail Works, which was situated there, was the first nail factory in the United States. In 1813, Lewis Wernwa, a bridge builder, became part owner of the factory and changed its name to the Phoenix Iron Works. In 1849, a new group of owners incorporated it as the Phoenix Iron Co., the same year the community was incorporated as a borough and renamed Phoenixville after the name of its major employer.

An important manufacturing center in its industrial heyday early in the twentieth century, Phoenixville was the site of great iron and steel mills such as the Phoenix Iron Works, boiler works, silk mill, underwear and hosiery factories, a match factory, and the famous (and now highly collectible) Etruscan majolica pottery.

More importantly, like many American towns and cities, Phoenixville owes its growth and sustenance to its waterways. It is not only situated on the broad Schuylkill River, a historic thoroughfare for Native Americans and early settlers alike, but it is bisected by the fast-flowing French Creek, which was quickly harnessed for water power.

And like many American towns, the waterways were used not only for industrial and business purposes, but for recreational activities as well.

By humans, animals, and creatures of the deep alike.

FLYNN'S GEESE

It had all started, according to the newspaper article that appeared on the front page of *The Evening Phoenix* on April 1, 1978, on the early morning of Thursday, March 30, 1978 when Flynn O'Rourke discovered that three of his prized geese had been slaughtered.

According to his account, he had heard faint grunting and groaning about an hour before dawn. Then he heard loud honking and chickens cackling. Clearly, he thought, the birds were agitated, but it was probably the thunder and lightening of a powerful rain storm that was quickly advancing on the area. He had hoped it was nothing more than that and rolled over onto his side to catch another wink or two of sleep before yet another long, grueling day running the dairy began. But when the grunting grew louder and the honking and cackling turned to screeching, he got up and pulled on his green denim overalls.

"What...what is it, dear?" his wife muffled from under the handmade quilt.

"Nothing, Kathleen." He tried to keep his voice calm. She was the nervous, jittery type; frightened by anything, everything out of the ordinary. No sense in upsetting her if it was, as he thought, yet another fox. "Probably just the thunder claps is what's got them rattled. I'll go check anyway."

He grabbed the double-barreled shotgun he kept loaded and leaning against the nightstand by the side of the bed and raced down the steps and out the door.

Feathers, feet, wings, and bits of flayed flesh were strewn all over the barnyard of his twenty-acre farm sprawled just below Mingo along the east bank of the Schuylkill River.

He knew it couldn't have been the vixen whom he had shot coming out of the henhouse the onset of last winter, nor her three kits who were so young they could not have survived the cold, harsh Phoenixville weather without her.

It surely wasn't Sean Conner's rambunctious Irish setter, either. Curly had been kept tethered up in the backyard ever since the last incident with Morgan Grant's young shepherd bitch who seven weeks later whelped such ugly puppies that when weaned they couldn't be sold. Morgan had to beg families all over upper Chester and lower Montgomery counties to take them in.

Nor could it have been the rogue cougar. It was last seen in these parts of eastern Pennsylvania two years ago, now presumed by the local authorities to have moved on.

No. The killing had to have been done by something, somebody else. But by what? By whom?

Now, Flynn had an intensely interesting face. With its deep crags of tanned, weather-beaten skin it looked lived in. Fierce deep blue eyes pierced out from under graying bushy brows. He was tall, lanky, with sinewy muscles rippling through his Chambray work shirt. While he presented a stern countenance to a passing stranger, he was actually a kind-hearted, considerate man. Except when his dander was fired up; this, him being Irish, didn't take much. He was known to rant and rage for hours, screaming at anyone, anything in his way.

Like on this cool, rainy morning when the air tinged with the acrid odor of blood and the crisp smell of approaching snow, belying the fact that the spring equinox was just last week. With the remains of his cherished and carefully raised blue-ribbon birds at his feet, it didn't feel anything like spring to Flynn. It felt more like the onslaught of a harsh winter once again.

Slamming open its wide wooden doors, he stormed into the barn and paced up and down the four-stall double-wide aisles checking to make sure the other animals – a dozen or so pigs, three horses, and a goat – were okay. They were. Frightened, he sensed, but still okay. He looked out the back of the lower hay mow. The herd of twenty or so cows out in the upper pasture began to amble toward the large barn. They seemed to be fine, too.

The horses neighed and nickered at him, welcoming his company. The pigs oinked and grunted, oblivious to their surroundings.. The goat, free to roam the barn, clambered up onto hay bales, whinnying loudly as if she had something urgent to tell him. The cows paced back and forth outside the dairy door, waiting to be milked and fed.

Flynn angrily fed his animals and then let the cows in, hooking each one up to the milking machine. He placed hay and feed before them and switched on the milker. It started to pulse. Streams of white were pumped through plastic tubes and flowed into the three refrigerator tanks in the pasteurizing room.

Later, Kathleen would come out after breakfast to do the processing, separating out the cream for butter and bottling the whole milk for delivery to the newly opened Redner's Market on upper Starr Street. It and Forresta's off North Bridge were the O'Rourke Dairy's best customers; from whom it made the most profit. With Easter approaching – only nine days away – they were sure to want double, perhaps triple orders of everything.

But Flynn would think about that later. After the

farm chores were done, and the cows were ambling back to pasture, he had a chance to begin to calm down and assess the damage.

He had had four gaggles of pure white Emden geese, housed in a large rookery that bordered one side of the fenced barnyard. They were the largest and most docile of the species, with snow white feathers, brilliant orange beaks, and speckled feet. They were, in Flynn's mind, the prettiest.

And while they were known for their quiet, almost human-like nature, the farmer raised them not as pets, but for the eggs, feathers, and holiday meat, replenishing the gaggles with the new hatchlings each summer. Although they were part of the family's dairy business, Flynn was quite saddened, as well as angry, to have lost three of them.

He entered the long, low building and counted to make sure there were twenty-five geese remaining.

There were.

He glanced at the blood and slime on the lintel of a hatch door. Whatever, whoever had pried it open and obviously reached in and one by one dragged out three of the males. Two of them were last year's Blue Ribbon winners at the State Farm Fair held each January in Harrisburg. The other was his daughter's favorite. Charles the First, whom she had raised since he first hatched out of his speckled egg. She would be more than upset when she found out Charlie had been murdered.

Thank goodness, he sighed, no more geese were slaughtered. From the looks of the remains, Flynn surmised, whoever, whatever, had probably eaten its full, taken what remained, and then wandered off.

He scoured the area for tracks, but the cascading rain had turned most of the yard into puddles of mud. If there had been prints, they were now obscured. While it seemed fruitless, Flynn angrily paced around the fence parameter anyway. Partly to search for clues, but more so to settle his temper.

At the far end of the barnyard, closest to the river, he found a deep groove, nearly four feet wide, in the muddy ground heading down to the water. More feathers were strewn on either side of it. He first assumed whoever had taken the geese had used a boat, but then dismissed the idea. There weren't any human footprints in the mud. Just the deep groove that looked like the smooth inner tube of a large rubber tractor tire had been rolled through it.

Dissatisfied there weren't any more clues or traces, he set about cleaning up the rest of the fowl remains.

He thought it best if his wife, when she came out to process the milk, didn't see what had happened. Actually, he didn't want her to know what had happened at all. But how would he keep the secret from his darling Kat?

His daughter, however. Well, that would be a different story. She would know something was wrong the very moment she came out later that afternoon to collect the eggs. He thought he should tell her before she left for school, but thought better of it. No sense upsetting her now. He was a protective father and he didn't want to ruin her day.

He cleaned up the yard as best he could, hoping the rain would wash away the rest. Then he went in to breakfast. Trying not to show how upset he was, he joked with his daughter and teased his wife. Then, to Kathleen's surprise, helped wash and dry the dishes. As they worked together, side-by-side, she refrained from asking what had disturbed the geese and chickens. Also a protective husband, he, too, refrained from offering any information.

After breakfast, he feigned an excuse to go into town for some supplies. Instead of driving over to the Tarrytowne Hardware store and mini-mall off Township Line Road, he went to the cinder block and steel Phoenixville Police Station on the east end of Bridge Street to report the incident. If someone was stealing fowl from his and neighboring farms, they ought to know – and do – something about it.

He stormed into the lobby, which was where Kelly

Pearce, an aspiring reporter on the staff of the local newspaper, just happened to be, perusing the police blotter for the day's news.

Not quite a Lois Lane looking for her Superman, she was as serious and eager. She was just beyond the cusp of earning a reputation for having a "nose for news," never missing a chance to turn the slightest observation into a full-fledged human interest feature story.

Lately, however, she was aiming for a bit more. A hard-core news story. One that, this time, would put her name under a large heading; a byline on the front page. It would be her first. In her pursuit, she didn't miss a trick. Everything she saw or heard, everyone she met...all were potential leads for what she would term "the Phoenixville news story of the year".

Kelly watched as Flynn O'Rourke strode purposefully into the station, an angry scowl on his weather-worn, lived-in face.

"Well, hi, there, Mr. O'Rourke," the police officer on duty smiled. "Nice to see you again so soon."

"This isn't another social call, Vicki," he grunted, glancing at the reporter. "Someone, something killed my geese!"

"All of them?"

"No, just three...but still...they were my geese."

"Tell me about it," the sergeant asked.

Kelly stood quietly beside Sergeant Vicki Henderson. She could feel his anger welling up inside him as she carefully listened to O'Rourke tell his story.

"Feathers and geese meat all over the place…Someone needs to come out and see that groove. It was not a boat, that's for sure," he said while Vicki jotted down a few notes.

"Very suspicious, Mr. O'Rourke," she said. "I'll dispatch someone to the dairy this afternoon to investigate. Okay?"

"Thanks," he said, storming out the door. He paused, and then turned. "Um, sorry to be so rude, but…It's good to see you again, too, Vicki."

Kelly wasn't sure, but she thought she saw on his craggy face, underneath all that anger, a glint of a smile.

"Who do you think the perp might be?" Kelly asked when the farmer had told his tale and then left. She reveled in talking what she termed "cop slang", trying to impress the policewoman, her new friend, with her savvy. Anything to get a good story.

"I don't think it was a human who slaughtered those geese. At least not anyone from around here,"

Sergeant. Henderson stated. "Mr. O'Rourke is highly respected in this community and, well, with his black Irish temper, I doubt anybody would even dare enter his barnyard without his permission. Let alone kill any of his livestock. Nope...don't think so."

"Then who, er, what do you think it would be?"

"Don't know," the sergeant mused. She mocked a menacing face. "Maybe a monster, perhaps? Who knows? Guess we'll have to send someone out to Mingo to look into it."

Kelly's ears perked up.

"A monster, you say?"

"Yeah, could be," Vicki teased, dropping her professional persona and lapsing into her dry, Germanic sense of humor. "A big, hungry monster from the river," she chuckled.

"Interesting." Kelly said. She uncapped her ballpoint pen and began taking notes on a fresh page of her steno pad, already half-full with musings, leads, and article ideas.

She sensed this might be the hard-core news lead she was looking for. It had to be. The eager, serious-minded reporter felt it in her bones.

"Say, Vicki. Can I quote you on that?"

BLACK ROCK DAM

Black Rock Dam, located between Phoenixville and Mingo on the Schuylkill River, is a low head dam. It does not completely block the river, but slows its flow downstream from Royersford and Spring City through Phoenixville. As water cascades over the top of the dam, it forms small, foaming eddies below that twist and turn for another quarter mile or so, then undulates gently as it courses downstream, feeding the canal parallel to Lock 60 with smooth waters.

Also known as Black Rock Run Dam, the structure spans across the river at a relatively narrow point. Originally constructed as a stone filled, timber crib dam in the early 19th century by the Schuylkill Navigation Company, the dam was used first used in 1825, one of dozens built to create slack water pools for the canal system of which Lock 60 is a part. It was later rebuilt with concrete blocks.

In the mid-1880s the canal system constituted the major means of transporting the wealth of resources from the rich coal fields and lush farm soils of inner Pennsylvania to the burgeoning city of Philadelphia and beyond. But by the late 1880s, railroads started making inroads carrying both passengers and freight to and from just about every major city and small village in the Keystone State. Trains were faster, cheaper, and could move goods and people much more quickly than barges pulled by mules down rivers. A line running along the eastern shore of the river soon caused the demise of the Schuylkill Canal System and, in the first quarter of the Twentieth Century, all that was left were the canal, the dam, and the lock.

Trout season wouldn't start that year until the Sunday after Easter; almost a week and a half away. Yet, Casey Seymour was up and at 'em early that rainy Friday morning, standing on the west bank of the Schuylkill River just below Black Rock Dam, his fly reel poised to be deftly flicked into the swiftly flowing waters sluicing over it.

Even though the catching might be sparse – the local gaming commission hadn't yet stocked the streams with troutlets as they do every spring – he figured he'd get a jump on the other borough fishermen.

Rainy weather always meant good fishing, he thought. Today was going to be good day. Maybe he'd catch a whopper for his dinner.

The sun had just begun to rise through the mists over the crest of trees along the upper part of the far bank when Casey cast his first fly of the day. It landed perfectly. Exactly where he had aimed it. In the shallows, just inside a slight bend in a narrow part of the river. Taking up the slack, he stepped off the bank and waded a bit into the water. He slowly counted to ten before reeling in and casting out again.

It was then the normally swift, but smooth waters above the dam began to churn and boil. A sharp loud grunting sound pierced through the distant thunder that gently, slowly rumbled across the hills on the opposite shore.

Startled, Casey looked up and was amazed to see what seemed to be the head of a giant serpent on a thick, wide neck appear over the crest of the dam. It twisted and turned, swiveling like a giant submarine periscope, as if it scanning the banks for something it had lost.

Or would want to attack.

Casey couldn't quite make out whether it had eyes or not. He honestly thought it all was just a trick of the sun glinting through the rain or the shadow of a branch of one of the massive sycamore trees that lined the river. Branches don't have eyes, he reasoned. Just knots and gnarls. Inanimate, they cannot see. Nor react. But when the "head" turned and stared straight at him, Casey knew it wasn't any large tree limb or a dark shadow.

He watched as a black hole slowly squeezed into a squint.

"That damned thing winking at me?" Casey asked out loud. But he didn't wait to find out. He suppressed a scream and quickly reeled in, scrambling up the bank away from the river. When he reached the crest of the steep hill, he turned around and watched as the giant head and thick neck moved toward the dam, backed away as if thwarted, then moved toward it again.

"Damn, it's almost as if it's sussing it out," Casey whispered. "As if planning an attack. Trying to overcome the obstacle in its way."

Disgusted, frightened, yet fascinated, Casey continued to watch the creature until it swam up river towards the wooden boating pier just below Spring City. He was about to continue up the bank when he heard a loud, low bellow. A cross between the screech of an injured elephant and the roar of an angry grizzly. He turned back toward the river and again watched as the large, grey-green scaled head and neck sailed back toward the dam, picking up more speed as it came downstream.

"Hell-bent for leather," Casey said out loud, trying to stay calm. But he couldn't.

"God, that thing is surely ugly. Green scales and slime all over. Aaaarrgggh."

Casey was sickened by the sight, from the fear welling up in his belly. He bent over, hands on his thighs, head between his knees. He vomited what little was left of the fried egg sandwich he had had for breakfast, and then wiped his month with the heel of his hand.

Afraid, yet also too fascinated to continue trudging up the hill, he stood stock still as the monster raised out of the water, placed two front flippers squarely on top of the dam and, to his amazement, vaulted over.

It was in the spewing foam below the dam. Then, just as Casey blinked, it dove under water. He watched the wake as it swam past the canal and Lock 60, heading at a rapid clip downriver.

"I gotta tell someone about this," he muttered, trying to remember where he had parked his Jeep. He knew if he went to the police he'd be reported to the county game warden for poaching fish out of season.

Instead, when he got back to his small wood-framed house on Norwood Street in Mont Clare, he called the local newspaper.

"It looked like the thing was swimming downstream," he told Kelly Pearce, the avid reporter who took what the receptionist called a "crank call".

She was excited. It was a second incident; the first-time sighting. Her story was escalating from a back page blurb to her coveted front page story.

"Then it became blocked by the dam," Casey said, as Kelly furiously typed out notes on the Royal typewriter, the phone receiver cupped between her chin and the top of her left shoulder. "By golly, if it didn't did turn and look directly at me," he explained. "I even thought it winked at me, but it might have been..."

"Dawn sunlight reflecting on mists rising up from the water?" Kelly suggested, knowing full-well that it probably wasn't.

"Might have. I don't know. I didn't stick around long enough to find out. But, I tell ya, the damn thing sure looked like some kind of monster. Yet," he added as an afterthought, "I could 'a sworn it winked at me."

Not only a monster, as Vicki had suggested earlier, Kelly smiled to herself, but a flirtatious one at that.

When she asked how to spell Casey's name so she could quote him properly, the caller quickly hung up.

"Game wardens are one thing," Casey said to himself, panting heavily. "But that thing was too much."

Kelly decided this story was good enough to talk to the features editor about later that afternoon.

"Hell no. With murdered geese and a frightened fisherman, this is no feature," she said, beginning to write an outline for her article. "It's hard-core news. Maybe I'd better talk to Nancy."

WATER TREATMENT PLANT

The Valley Forge Sewer Authority plant that serviced not only Phoenixville, but the surrounding communities of upper Valley Forge, Kimberton, and the eastern part of Schuylkill Township, sat on fifty-four secluded acres on the other side of Phoenixville proper, just two miles from the back entrance of the newly re-named Valley Forge National Park, Built in 1969 with five huge treatment and holding tanks, it was perfectly situated on the confluence of the Schuylkill River and Perkiomen Creek at the lower end of Route 29, with easy access to both waterways.

Across the street, adjacent to Pawlings Road, rose a spillway dam that kept a large reservoir, filled by fresh spring water from Pickering Creek, at bay. Overflow water from the reservoir cascaded over the dam, filling two sluices that coursed under Valley Forge Road feeding three of the plant's tanks.

About a half hour before lunch, Jimmy Sturgeon, the operator of the water treatment plant, walked out onto one of steel girder catwalks over the waste tanks to catch a smoke. Just as he lit a Marlboro he heard thrashing in one of the sluices.

Curious, he took a long drag of his cigarette,

flicked it over the railing, and ambled to the bank to see what was going on.

An enormous shadow snaked its way through the top of the sluice as it emerged from under the side of the road and stopped. It kept thrashing and the water kept churning.

"The rain had abated a bit and there, for a few moments, it was as clear as a sunny day," he told Sergeant Vicki Henderson, the police officer who had come later that afternoon to investigate.

One of the three female police officers newly-appointed three months ago to the force, Vicki was, like the two other women who were hired the same time she was, trying all too hard to make an impression on their male counterparts. In her efforts, despite her droll, witty, often prankish sense of humor when not on duty – although sometimes it did slip out and get her into a bit of trouble while in uniform – she took just about everything way too seriously. It was an innate trait she was trying very hard to overcome.

"What, exactly did you see?" she asked, lowering her voice in an attempt to be officious. She took out a small leather-bound notebook and clicked a red Parker T-ball Jotter once, twice, three times in anticipation. Despite being serious, she knew that she'd have to conduct this investigation with two or more grains of salt. Or maybe, instead, a teaspoon of sugar.

"Well,'" Jimmy continued. "It looked like the water in the upper end of the sluice was boiling. Actually boiling. Like a mad tea kettle. Bubbles, churning. Waves all over the place. Sort of like there was something under the water swimming. No," he paused, "like something was desperately struggling to get free."

"Could you identify it? You know, surmise what it might be?"

"The water is a bit murky there, what with the waste and all, so I couldn't quite make it out. I thought I saw a large shadow at one point. Kinda slithery. Whatever it was, it would have to be huge to create that kind of violence in the water."

Jimmy fell silent as the policewoman jotted down a few words in her notebook. He lit up a Marlboro and leaned against a railing, trying to look casual and cool like the bronzed cowboy in the commercials. But Jimmy's face, given what he had seen that morning, was as white as a frenzied specter newly released from limbo.

He tired to distract himself by smoking and, God help him, ogling the woman. She was, as policewomen go, with her closely cropped curly red hair and infectious smile, quite pretty. He couldn't help but notice small, perky breasts straining against the light blue blouse of her one-size-too-small uniform.

Maybe, he thought, after she's finished with all her questions, I'll ask her out for a drink.

"Anything else?" Vicki asked, carefully watching Jimmy's face as it turned ashen, then reddened. Then turned pale again. She, of course, had no idea what his inner thoughts were. So taken was she with doing her job correctly – "by the book" – she forgot her own feminine wiles and their mesmerizing effect on men. Ever since she was a little girl and learned by herself how to flirt with the young boys growing up on South Street.

What she desired most of all at that moment was a slew of clues to piece together to solve this almost ludicrous case and show Captain Paderewski that she was, in fact, detective material.

Maybe this guy is just a jester, a liar, a high-faluting self-centered fraud, she thought to herself. Just look at him standing there, smoking. Trying to be cool. Smug. Above it all.. Just like a few of the guys on the force who take their authority all to seriously. Who think more highly of themselves than the welfare of the community they are called upon to serve.

She thought back upon her first interview with Captain Marcos Paderewski, the week after she had graduated from the Philadelphia Police Academy.

He had been impressed with her high marks that were hard-earned at the academy and sterling recommendations from some of the instructors. Yes, as she explained, even with the marks and comments, she was unable to secure a position on the city's squad under Mayor Frank Rizzo's strict, misogynistic administration.

"I thought I'd take a crack, er, a stab here in the suburbs," she said.

"We'd love to have you," the Captain slowly remarked, stooping over a copy of her school records and résumé. "But first I have to get the Borough Council's approval."

It took the better part of a month, but, finally, after a few trials and tribulations – and passing the rigorous physical and showing her mettle during a mock-trial "emergency" – she had landed a coveted Sergeant's post in, of all places, the sleepy town of Phoenixville, Chester County, PA.

By all accounts it was a decent job and rank. Good pay. Clean air. She was able to rent a nice apartment off Route 113 in a large complex with a pool and two tennis courts. But, still, it wasn't her first choice: the prestigious Philadelphia Police force. And, although boasting it was one of "the preferred suburban places to live," it definitely was not downtown Philly. Not even South Street.

"Um, well...I stood over there." Jimmy said, interrupting her thoughts. He pointed to the spot on the bank that sloped to the junction of the sluice with the reservoir outlet. "I watched for a while. Watching the thrashing and boiling...Then...then..." he took another long drag on his cigarette.

"Then? What then?"

"Well...It looked like fins. Large, grey fins...like on a shark or a dolphin, you know? Coming right out of the sluice. They broke the water, like a whale flipping over. Like in the movie, Moby Dick...Ya know?"

"I've heard of it. Yes..." She continued to jot notes.

"I guessed at first that it was a large fish...or something...swimming to the surface to avoid the turbulence. But that it wasn't it that was making the water churn."

"Did you see a head, perhaps? Maybe a tail? Anything else?"

"Um, no." Another drag, flicking ashes into one of the waste materials holding tanks. "Just the fins. So it must have been a...big...um, a big fish. Yeah, that's what it was. A big fish."

"Well, then. Not a monster." Sergeant Vicki sighed disappointingly. No case here. "Just a big fish. Um, okay," she stated flatly. A big fish tale, she said to herself, smiling wanly at the pun.

"I guess that's it. Nothing more than maybe one of those large, monster catfish everyone's talking about that got caught in your sluice. I'll just call this in and consider this 'case closed'." She flipped down the lid of the notebook and clicked the Jotter three more times to retract the nib. As Jimmy closely watched, she stuffed them both into the left breast pocket of her uniform blouse. Then she turned her back to go. She was, obviously, annoyed.

Too obviously annoyed.

Obviously annoyed with him.

He scuffed his shoe against the grating and reached for another cigarette.

"Sorry to have wasted your time," Jimmy called to her, trying to apologize as she strutted up the catwalk to the white and dark blue squad car. He flicked the remains of the Marlboro onto the grimy grid and ground them out with the toe of his waders.

Disgusting, he thought. This place is filthy. He'd have to get one of the workers who swabbed out the empty waste tanks every week to also clean the girder decks.

"No problem. Sorry to have wasted yours." She flicked a backhanded wave, flashed a weak smile he did not see, and continued on.

"Yeah, right." Jimmy sighed. "No chance now I'll

get to ask her out."

He lit another cigarette, trying to figure out what had just happened. And what had happened before.

What he saw wasn't a big fish, as he so off-handedly and all too quickly suggested. No way in hell it was.

"I know it wasn't," he breathed out with a lungful of smoke. "A monster? As the sergeant seemed to think. Maybe?" He chuckled. "Who knows what strange things lurk in the sluices of waste plants?" He took another drag. "Maybe the shadow do," he quipped, flicking the still-burning cigarette into the holding tank below his feet.

"And I do know this," he promised out loud, "it weren't any shadow. I have to figure out what it really was and tell her. And, perhaps, then, there'd be another chance to ask her out..."

AT THE VALE-RIO

Long since replaced by an all pink ice cream parlor, the Vale-Rio Diner back in its hay day in 1978 was not only "the" local eatery serving hearty breakfasts and traditional all-American luncheon fare, but also doubled as Phoenixville's most popular community center. Primarily frequented by the older generation, it was also a favorite daytime hangout for some of the younger residents, as well. Particularly the local police, who would stop in for a quick cup of Joe while on patrol.

Originally, it was a railroad dining car that was hauled on wheels into town by mules borrowed from local bargemen who plied their trade up and down the Schuylkill Canal System. It took two weeks for the river workers to set it upon a cinder block foundation next to the Fountain Inn, on the corner of Nutt Road and West Bridge Street.

The intersection was once known as the "Western Gateway to Valley Forge", marked by a monument indicating that it was the farthest point that was reached by British forces during the Revolutionary War.

Over the years, the Vale-Rio's dull brownish

green exterior and sleek leather and shiny brass interior décor had been replaced with a gleaming blue and silver façade and, at the time of its second refurbishing, modern appliances and overstuffed vinyl counter stools, cushioned booths, and roomy banquettes.

It was rumored to have been one of the Phoenixville locations in the 1958 movie, *The Blob*, starring a young Steve McQueen in the roll of an overly zealous teenager battling to save his hometown from being absorbed by a mass of green jelly-like substance. But even as the rumors proved false – a diner in Coatesville was used, instead – the Vale-Rio was still a thriving Mecca for tourists and residents alike.

Famous for its open-faced beef or turkey sandwiches, triple-decker BLTs, crispy fires, fire-broiled hamburgers, and Celeste's own special western omelets, residents of Chester and Montgomery counties – and beyond – flocked to partake of its down-home fare as well as its down-to-earth atmosphere.

The Vale-Rio was, in its day, a true, treasured icon of Americana. Phoenixville style.

Around lunchtime on any given early afternoon, a cadre of retired, older locals would gather, filling up the booths and counter stools, to eat while savoring items read out loud from the previous day's issue of *The Evening Phoenix*, which, despite its name, was on the newsstands and delivered on people's porches and doorsteps by three or four o'clock in the afternoon. No later, to some places in and around the borough, including Seacrist's and the magazine rack in Redner's, than five.

The diner's regulars – mostly retirees from the steel plant, the hospital, and the former Valley Forge General Hospital whose campus was now occupied by the local Christian college – would typically read their paper after dinner. After the city's television newscasts that brought them the national and international news had signed off, they would pore over the seven or eight pages, noting with avid interest the more salient stories that would be the next day's topics of conversation.

Then, just before lunch time – a few of the retirees even ventured out for breakfast – they'd don loose-fitting chinos and golf shirts or pastel, bodice-sequined sweat suits (depending upon gender) and head on over to the Vale-Rio, cramming into the blue vinyl booths, munching on the day's specials, reading and commenting upon items in the previous day's paper.

Occasionally, a fellow resident or village employee would stop in with a juicy tidbit or two to share before it hit that night's *The Evening Phoenix*. Most of the Vale-Rio regulars savored these stories. They reveled in having a head start, a jump on the news long even before the local reporters even got wind of them.

On the afternoon of March 30th, Sergeant Henderson stopped by the diner on her way back from the treatment plant and chatted with a few of the local regulars as she ate her early dinner BLT and chocolate shake at the counter. She had, recalling how he had looked at her, asked Celeste, working the counter that shift, about Jimmy Sturgeon.

"Well, with those deep brown eyes of his and his long, tall, cool, tanned glass-of-milk build, he's not that half bad a looker, either," Celeste teasingly said, clearing dirty plates away and putting them into a large galvanized rubber bin under the counter.

"Is he, um, married? Going with anyone?"

"Not that I know of. Seems to be a bit of a...How shall I say? A ladies man, if you know what I mean. Why? Are you interested?"

"Not sure. The way he was, um, ogling me when I was asking questions and writing down about what he saw in the sluice...Acting cool. Pretending to be in a cigarette commercial. I might be. He amuses me," the policewoman grinned."

"Well, I'd tread cautiously," the waitress advised.

She paused thoughtfully, wiping down the counter with a damp dish towel. "What did he see in the sluice, honey?"

Celeste, a long time part-owner of the diner, was always up for a juicy tidbit of newsy gossip. Anything to cut through the thick layer of boredom that often hovered during the occasionally slow days at work. Despite it being a popular "eat-at-Joe's" joint, it did have its rare lull periods.

"Some large shadow with fins, churning up the water," the sergeant ventured." She smiled. "Probably another big catfish that Mr. Montoya occasionally catches to feed his brood. But, you know, I can't say anything more. Until we find out what it really was." She sighed. "Well, it's police business….and all that."

"Sure, hon. But I'd be wary of anyone seeing things out of the ordinary on the job. Wasn't drinking, was he?"

"No. I don't think so. I mean, he doesn't usually drink, does he?"

"Only casually at the Columbia on its Thursday all-you-can-eat buffet nights. Sometimes on Friday. But never alone. He's usually with his buddies." Celeste winked. "Male buddies. Never alone," she reiterated.

"Well, I'll just have to check that out," Vicki winked back as she put a ten-spot on the counter to cover her lunch. "Thanks for the tip," she punned. "And keep the change."

The counter waitress waited until Vicki had left and was crossing the parking lot to the police car. When she was sure the policewoman was safely behind the wheel and about to pull out into traffic, Celeste slapped her dirty towel hard on the counter.

"I knew she was coming in here to tell me something special!" she said to herself. "Hey, folks, you'll never guess what that imaginative Jimmy Sturgeon saw swimming in the treatment plant this morning," she then called to no one and everyone in particular. "Some kind of river beast, churning up the waters..."

"Must be the thing that got O'Rourke's geese..." a gruff-faced customer called from a booth.

"And Topper's cow," another smirked.

"Be careful, Sam," Celeste grinned back, not questioning how they already knew what Vicki had just told her. News, especially juicy news, travelled fast in the steel town. "Ain't this how false rumors get started?"

"Wouldn't know about that...But we got ourselves a real, true mystery here,. Don't we, fellows?"

Everyone, talking amongst themselves, agreed.

"Maybe somebody ought to call that Kelly Pearce down at the paper," Sam laughed again. "She's pretty industrious, that one. Always snooping around our business for a story or two. She'll get to the murky bottom of it, for sure."

"That a pun, Sam?" another customer sitting at the far end of the counter swilling cold coffee and contemplating the slice of lemon meringue pie in front of him. "If it is, it's a mighty poor one." He paused. "But knowing Sergeant Vicki there and her antics…I somehow think that reporter already knows all about it."

"Yeah, I reckon she does," came a voice from someone hiding in a booth along the row of windows facing Bridge Street. No one could see his face, still ashen with fear. The tenor voice rose slightly above a whisper as Casey Seymour began to relate what he saw that morning while fishing.

"Yeah, I was out early this morning to get me a bass or a trout for dinner," he admitted. He was sure there weren't any game wardens in the diner that day.

And, if they were, to hell with 'em.

Celeste's customer's ears picked up, eager to hear what the man had to say. She smiled. Another scoop for the crowd.

One portly older gentleman, who had just buried his wife in Morris Cemetery a few short days ago, jumped off his counter stool and ambled down the narrow diner aisle to sit squarely opposite the wayward fisherman in his booth.

"Go-wan," Lenny Leighton urged, eager for a diversion from the boring prospect of living his remaining years alone without the understanding companionship and almost denigrating servitude of Leah, his beloved wife.

They had been married for forty-five years. Leah's death of undetected lung cancer – Stage Four by the time the doctor thought to do a blood test for what he had previously claimed was "nothing more than a persistent cold" – was so totally devastatingly unexpected.

Leah had lasted for a year, struggling against the cruel side-effects of chemotherapy, mourning with her husband the loss of her life even before it had ended. She had, however, gratefully died in his arms. She had remained there for more than a day before Lenny thought to call Klotzbach's Funeral Home to finally take her away.

Ever since they both retired from teaching third graders at Barkley Elementary School on 2nd Avenue Lenny and Leah had been coming to the Vale-Rio every day for lunch. As far as Celeste could recollect, that had to have been at least ten years ago. Her son, Billy, was still a sober, industrious kid back then. She shook her head to flip the memory of him as a teenager out of her mind and concentrated on Lenny.

Leah's death was, as he constantly replied when asked how he doing, "....not at all fair". But then, as he had often told his inquisitive students, "Prepare yourself. Nothing much in life is."

Lenny leaned across the grey and white marbled table, his reddening, arthritic hands clasped tightly in front of him. "Please do. Tell us more."

"That thing Jimmy saw, musta been the same thing I saw. With fins – a scaly green head atop a thick, long neck. By gum, it jumped right out of the water and over Black Rock Dam when I was there."

"Go away," Lenny jeered, quizzing Casey as if he was back standing up in front of one of his classes of squirming children. The fisherman, now one of his students. "You gotta be joking. Tell the truth, young man. Tell us the truth."

"No, no. I won't lie. I saw it with my own eyes. Looked right into the two black holes in its head. It even winked at me."

"I'll be," sighed the customer with the meringue pie, pushing the plate away. "Sorry, Celeste. It looks good, but now I think I've lost my taste for it.

"Yep. Sure as I'm sitting here," Casey continued. "It musta swum all the way down to the treatment plant and got caught in the sluice. A real monster."

"Well, I'll be damned," Lenny said. He caught himself before saying, "Wait until I tell Leah about this."

"I wonder if it managed to get out?" Celeste wondered. "Poor thing. Trapped like that."

Everyone knew she had a soft spot for all of God's living creatures.

Even if one was, as everyone in the Vale-Rio Diner that day were now calling it, a river monster.

AT THE POLICE STATION

Back at the station typing up her notes into a formal police report, Sergeant Vicki Henderson couldn't help but chuckle to herself.

So far, it was turning out to be a rather good day; one of the better ones she had so far had in her short, but lengthening career as an officer on the Borough of Phoenixville's police force.

She laughed out loud when she thought about the early morning guffaw with her friend, the all-too-eager reporter.

"What's so funny," the Chief called ponderously from his office. "Is there a joke you're not going to tell me? One I haven't heard yet?"

Vicki looked up from the report she was writing and attempted to smile an apology through the opaque glass that separated Marcos Paderewski's office from the squad's working area. He stood up, as best he could with his slumped shoulders and aggressive arthritis, and slowly sauntered over to the desk at which the sergeant was working.

With his slight frame and twisted build, Marcos Paderewski was stoop-shouldered. A mere comma of a man paused in the mid-sentence of life, as if to catch a breath or to ponder upon a bit of reflection before moving on. A more thoughtful, slow-paced man than a doer, it was nearly an enigma how he got to be Phoenixville's police chief. One would think a more dynamically aggressive, sterner looking man would be the more appropriate candidate. But, with his crossbred Spanish and Nordic heritage, the Borough Council had decided he had the tenacity, the will, and the innate talent to succeed at anything he put his mind to.

Besides, the local newspaper had noted, reporting on his swearing-in ceremony five years earlier on the steps of the Bridge Street police station, he was, in fact, a good friend of Topper Reilly, an irascibly determined councilman.

When she first met the Chief of Police during her interview, Vicki had sized him up as not being the shiniest penny in the piggy bank. Or the freshest cruller in the donut box.

Priding herself on being an intellectual, she often recited Shakespeare or quoted from Charles Dickens when issuing tickets. Not that not being an intellectual went hand-in-hand with their profession, but officers of her ilk, rising up as quickly as she was, fresh in the ranks, were a rarity.

Chief Paderewski was, indeed, as Phoenixville police went, the norm. Yet, she couldn't fathom him not being able to spell "Othello". When she advised him that "all the world's a stage…" was a line from Hamlet, he thought she was kidding.

"Geez, Louise. And here I thought 'Hamlet' was some kind of fancy brunch dish," he had frowned at his obvious ignorance in the face of one of his underlings, the newest member of his force. Obviously, she was much brighter, much smarter then he ever was or ever would be.

The sergeant smiled, not sure whether his ignorance was feigned or real. She gave him the benefit of the doubt, attributing his comments to, perhaps, getting on in years. After all, wasn't it the rumor that he was close to retirement? Two, three, four years at the most and the Borough Council would be looking for a new candidate to fill the slot. If she worked hard enough. Proved herself. Might it not be her? And why not?

Yet, Paderewski was, indeed, tenacious and he was good at what he did. And, after all, he was her Chief. The better part of valor here, she reminded herself, was loyalty.

"No joke, Chief," Vicki said, raising one finger up and turning her head to one side, as if to quizzically ask if it he had time to chat with her.

"Yeah, yeah, come in. What's on your mind?"

"Well, there was this sighting…Actually two

sightings. One at the dam, another at the treatment plant..."

"What the hell are you talking about?" Chief Paderewski did not read the police blotter on a daily basis, as others on the force thought was part of his job. Instead, not that keen on reading – some thought he was quite mildly illiterate – he relied on brief verbal synopses of the police reports other officers wrote.

"The beast, the monster," the sergeant ventured. Chief Marcie-Marcos, as most of the women on the force called him, would be the one person who certainly wouldn't believe what she was about to tell him.

"What's the word? Pre-post-ter-ous," he said slowly, sounding out each syllable, not so much for emphasis, but more as if to understand what he, himself, was saying. Vicki couldn't fathom which. "That right?"

"Well, those who saw it...believe what they've seen," she countered, adjusting the front of her light blue uniform blouse. No wonder Jimmy gaped at her. There were two gaps between the row of buttons and the buttonhole placard. Time to get a new uniform, she mused. One size up. Maybe two. Damn Celeste's all too creamy and way too tasty chocolate shakes.

"What they tell us they seen and what we figure

out they really saw are two different things, Sergeant."

"Yes, sir."

"You getting to the bottom of this?"

"Certainly, sir," she said smartly. There was a respectful, yet wry salute in the tone of her voice.

"Good. Now go figure out what it was...is. I am counting on you."

She turned to go back to her desk.

"And, sergeant," he said quietly. "Please don't mention this to anyone. I don't want the citizens of this fair village rattled and scared by something that may turn out to be a hoax. Got that?"

"Yes, sir," she said, bowing in acquiescence to his command, half way hoping that her intended slip of the tongue at the Vale-Rio Diner wouldn't go any further than Celeste. Not until she actually knew what it was that Jimmy supposedly saw.

She smiled into her ill-fitting collar. Tomorrow, tomorrow, she thought, I'll have to call Redd's Uniform Supply and make an appointment for a fitting.

"Good," her Chief said. "Now, get out."

When she got back to her desk, Vicki called Kelly

at the paper.

"Please be in," she whispered to herself. "I don't think I can keep this in any longer."

The reporter answered on the third ring.

"Not sure if you might be interested in this..." the sergeant laughed into the receiver, "But we're friends and, well, I just had to tell you. You ready for this?"

"Go on," Kelly said, again cupping the phone receiver between her chin and collarbone. She rolled a new sheet of letter-sized newsprint into the platen. She poised her fingers poised over the typewriter keys. "Shoot."

"I was out at the treatment plant and...well, the operations manager – a rather cute, studily guy named Jimmy..."

"I know him."

"You do?"

"Yeah. This is a small town, ya know. He thinks he's the original Marlboro man..."

She refrained from explaining that they had dated two or three times, but that after the necking disaster in Memorial Park she had called their relationship off. She was too ambitious and he, she sighed when she told him, too laid back. Not serious enough to, well, take her and her career seriously.

Maybe Sergeant Vicki, with her wicked off-duty sense of duty might fare better with him. But Kelly dared not suggest it. At least not now, when she was hot on the trail of her all-important news-of-the-year story.

"Yeah, well. Whatever," Vicki grinned to herself. "He thinks he saw something...something huge rising out of the sluice that connects the reservoir with the holding tanks."

"What? Could it be? The, er, the, our 'monster'?" Kelly anxiously asked.

Her story was gaining momentum, getting even better and better. She looked at the map of Phoenixville on which she was tracking the times and places of incidents and sightings. So far, it – he? she?—had travelled from the Black Rock Dam all the way down to the treatment plant on the other side of town.

Impressive.

Amazing.

Where will it go next?

"Not sure, but he swears by the churning and long neck...And the fins. He actually saw fins rising out of the water like a whale's...Like in *Moby Dick*, he said. Could be a trick of...you know, a troupe d'oeil. But still..."

"Yeah, right. Not sure what that means, Vicki. But I am right on it. Gotta go. Thanks for calling...But..." She paused, remembering it would be rude to hang up so abruptly. "Can I catch up with you later?"

"Yeah, sure," the sergeant said. "Maybe a drink at the Columbia? I'll be off duty by six. I could sure use a Bloody Mary."

"Double dry martinis for me," Kelly said. "We could also partake of their all-you-can-eat buffet."

"Sure. Sounds like a plan."

"Then it's a date, my friend," Kelly smiled. She looked at the notes she had just typed from their conversation. Then up at the clock on the newsroom wall. It was nearly four. She had just two hours left of her own workday to finish her outline. Best she got to it. "Okay, then. Bye," she said, then hung up the phone.

"You're falling for this," the sergeant whispered to the definitive click and then the buzzing dial tone on the other end of the line. "Aren't you, my friend? Hook, line, and sinker."

GREEN SCALES

As the reports about the various strange occurrences and sightings in and around the Schuylkill River began to trickle and then flood in, Vicki's cohorts at the police station were not so sure that the "perpetrator" as they called the "huge thing," was not really just a big fish. Or even someone in a wide round bottom boat. These assumptions, the jumping to conclusions were, to more than just a few practical members of the twenty-five person force, just way too simple.

Some of the theories included a hungry drifter and the return of the cougar. But these did not explain the lack of footprints, despite the deluging rain, in O'Rourke's barnyard nor the shadow churning and thrashing in the water at the plant.

In light of the many divergent, yet similar developments in the course of that March 30th day since that first morning's incident on O'Rourke's farm, there had to be another, more complex explanation.

But what could, would, should it be?

"Perhaps," one patrolman suggested, "someone is playing a hoax?"

"Nope, that isn't it," Vicki said adamantly, trying

to suppress a giggle. "Why would anyone go to such trouble...and also kill innocent geese? If someone is playing a prank, that's going way too far. Don't worry," she smiled at the patrolman, sufficiently chastised by a superior officer. "I'll figure it out."

Chief Paderewski chided them all for loitering around the station and speculating. He – and they – had a village to patrol and residents to protect as he repeatedly reminded them throughout the afternoon.

"Yet," he did say slowly, looking at each of the member of the force in turn. "There is more to this than meets the eye."

"Give it a rest, everyone," he finally growled. "Sergeant Henderson has a handle on it. Give her what you got and let her do her job." He paused, thinking what to say next. "So you can go out and do yours."

In March of 1978, the Borough of Phoenixville was a bustling community, with a population of just a little less than 8,000. The majority of residents worked at the Phoenix Steel Corporation – originally the French Creek Nail Works – one of the village's top three employers. Even after more than 200 years in business, it was still going strong. The purveyors of many radical, ultra-modern industry-changing inventions, it had manufactured the hundreds of miles of steel cable that are still used today to pull cable cars up and down the hills of San Francisco.

Back in 1888, when it was the Phoenix Iron Company, its president, David Reeves, designed the Phoenix Column. His hollow wrought-iron circular column was a marvel at the time because, unlike other iron building components, it could be riveted. This enabled the construction of taller and taller buildings – skyscrapers that would not collapse under their own weight. He had plans of his own to build a 1,000-foot high observation tower solely constructed of his columns. The tower was never built, but his plans inspired Gustave Eiffel to build his own now-famous wrought-iron tower in Paris.

Workers – and residents – of the Phoenixville Steel Company were – and still are – proud of their contribution to the erection of many of the higher buildings and elevated trains in New York City, as well as buildings in Chicago, and, more importantly, in Philadelphia, their own backyard.

The massive forges and plants of the steel company comprised the better part of Phoenixville's downtown proper, commanding the large area between Bridge Street and the Schuylkill River that flowed unabashedly through the borough it edged to later connect further downstream with the Delaware River. The company workers were proud of their past and present contributions to the community and to the world beyond its borders.

As written in one feature article that appeared earlier in *The Evening Phoenix,* an editor noted that the Phoenixville connection with places all over the world "...continues to surprise and please us."

Billy Bushmill was aptly named, given his affinity for the Irish whiskey with the same name. He was the cagey, shifty sort and a bigger drunk than Topper Reilly. But, unlike Topper, he didn't have a designated seat or booth in any of the local bars. He, instead, preferred to drink alone out of a bottle perched on whatever Reeves Park bench he happened to be sitting or sleeping upon that day. Or night. Otherwise occupied with grander thoughts than Reilly would ever have, he spent hours alone guarding the small brown khaki duffel bag stuffed underneath the bench that contained all of his worldly possessions. And, unlike Reilly, he was also much younger, considerably poorer, and, while always full of hope, an even bigger fool.

Not quite thirty, he had been married and divorce three times; bankrupt twice; and, because of his constant drinking, was unable to keep the only decent job he had ever had,

At the steel plant he helped pour vats of molten iron into huge cauldrons, part of the Bessemer process to purify the raw metal. After the first three months, he was finally earning enough to rent one of the rooms in the Pennsylvania Hotel reserved for long-term residents. He was also drinking less.

Unfortunately, however, despite his big dreams, what little ambition he had was centered on being able to get up on time for work and to work hard enough to eventually be promoted to being one of the machine operators that were to work in the proposed tube finishing department, where long hollow shafts of steel were cut into varying lengths. The job, one of forty or so, would be less strenuous and far less dangerous than pouring molten metal. But Billy never did have much stamina, let alone tenaciousness.

His job lasted a little less than a year and four months until he slipped on a piece of slag and had to be taken to the emergency room at Phoenixville Hospital where he was treated for second and third degree burns on his left arm and back.

His recovery took longer than he and his employers expected. On disability for a while, he reverted to his old ways, spending most of his money on booze. When he failed to return to work after two months, the benefits ceased. When he failed to pay his rent on time, the hotel management kicked him out. Billy was back on the streets again.

The only one thing he had going for him, beside his various attempts to live by his wits – the seat of his worn, fraying pants, as it were – was his uncanny ability to always tell the truth. He was as honest, as the saying goes, as the day was...is long. Despite his heavy drinking, he had all his faculties and a fine memory, even when drunk. And he was never ashamed to remind the Phoenixville townsfolk of it.

So what he later related what he saw, or thought he saw, that mid-afternoon of March 30, while walking across the Pawlings Road Bridge that spanned a wider section of the Schuylkill just had to be believed. After all, the story was told by Honest Billy.

And it more than startled most of the police force.

As well as Kelly Pearce, the intrepid ace reporter whose hopes for a byline under a front page heading in 24-point Bodoni Bold were now becoming a near-future reality.

Now Celeste, part-owner of the Vale-Rio Diner, was Billy's mother. She wasn't too proud of the fact that her son was the borough's boozer. But, despite her efforts to reform him, there was nothing much she could do.

Except feed him.

Occasionally, Billy would stop in during her lunchtime shift and she'd cook up a special California burger and a plateful of fries for him. More than half the time, it was the only meal he'd eaten for that day. Or even for the next two or three days. His body was so acclimated to the grains in Bushmill's, it was able to sustain itself on the suspect nutrients alone. Billy claimed he was never really hungry, but had stopped into the diner just to assure his mother he was okay.

It was the least he could do.

On Wednesday, while munching his usual burger and fries, Celeste leaned over the counter and told him about a new job opening up at Jeff's Landscaping located just over the Pawlings Bridge, on the corner of Gertrude Avenue.

Across from the entrance to the River Trail, another of Billy's summertime sleeping places.

On the mornings he did slumber on one of the benches along the trail, he'd wander across the highway and stop in to bum a cup of coffee and a cigarette from Jeff. However, it being a damp, chilly spring, Billy hadn't frequented one of his favorite sleeping – and drinking – haunts since last August. Had he stopped in recently, he would have probably been told of the job by the landscaper himself. Not hear about it second-hand from his mother.

"I'm not one to dig in the dirt," Billy said, munching on a fry. After his stint at the Phoenix Steel Corporation, even though it didn't pan out like he wanted, he still felt he was destined for greater things.

"Ya don't need to dig in the soil," Celeste said. "Just occasionally shovel it. But Jeff – he was in here just this morning – told me he needed someone to help out with his various lawn mowing gigs. Doing edging. Even running the mowers. He asked if I knew of anyone..."

"And you thought of me?"

"Of course. You're my son, aren't you? Why wouldn't I think of you? Besides, you need a job."

"Don't know if I really do, Ma." He paused, thoughtfully swirling the last of his fries in a puddle of ketchup. "Although, running a lawn mower might be some kinda fun."

"There ya go," she grinned. "You can go see him tomorrow, after lunch. He's expecting you. Who knows? This may be a whole new career for you."

"Yeah," Billy said, crumpling up the paper napkin he had used to wipe burger juice and ketchup from his lips and chin and tossing it onto his empty plate.

If nothing else, he had learned, besides always to be honest, some manners from his mother.

"A new career," he chuckled. "Like I don't like the one I already got."

So, it was around two o'clock, maybe closer to two-thirty the next day, Thursday, when Billy, having concluded his business at Jeff's Landscaping, was walking back toward Valley Forge Road, crossing the two-lane Pawlings Road Bridge on the left-hand side. He was just about in the middle when he thought he saw a strange shadow moving upstream toward him.

The rain had abated for a half hour, giving Billy a relatively dry walk back to town. The sun tentatively peered out from behind a few puffy, grey clouds, affording him unobstructed scrutiny of the river. Billy stopped and leaned over the steel railing – probably made at the Phoenix Steel Corporation – facing down river to get a better view.

He squinted as he watched, certain his eyes weren't playing tricks on him. After all, in anticipation of working at Jeff's, he had only a few slugs of the Bushmill's the night before. He had slept off what little buzz he had in his sleeping bag in a storeroom of the treatment plant, so he'd be fresh in the morning. Jimmy, the daytime operator, was one of his buddies and often snuck Billy in before he closed up the plant for the night.

The 24-hour semi-abstinence paid off. He had gotten the job mowing lawns on the condition that he showed up sober every morning promptly at nine o'clock. No later than ten. Jeff knew Billy's reputation and patterns from his few-mornings-a-week summer visits – and having also been alerted by Celeste, the good-humored and kindhearted waitress at the diner. He liked Billy. Especially his honesty – telling it like it is. Jeff was willing to give Celeste's son the benefit of the doubt.

Billy was in a hurry to get back to the treatment plant to fetch his sleeping bag and canvas duffel. Maybe he could borrow twenty or so dollars from Jimmy to buy some dinner later; maybe even a pint of Bushmill's before that. He was in the mood to celebrate his good fortune, but couldn't do it without a bit of cash in his pocket.

Then he'd hitch a ride up Route 23 to the diner and give his mother the good news. He would ask to stay with her over the weekend – he was to start his job on Monday. Maybe longer until he could find a more permanent place to stay.

Billy contemplated his plans, eager to carry them out. But the shadow, now looming toward the bridge, had captured his attention. He watched as it propelled itself closer and closer, morphing from a large, dark blur in the water to a large, grey-green oblong shape that looked very much like the pictures and sketches he had seen years ago in elementary school.

When an ugly, scaly head perched upon a long, thick neck reared above the water, he knew instantly what it was.

"Oh, flame-broiled hockey pucks!" he swore under his breath. "It's a smaller version of Nessie, the Scottish monster of the deep."

Too frightened to move, Billy stood stock still, watching as the beast propelled itself with its muscled fins through the water under the bridge to the other side. Obviously, it was oblivious to anything above it, seemingly intent on following its own chosen path.

He watched in amazement as it disappeared under the stanchioned roadway. He then dodged traffic to be on the other side of the bridge where he watched the monster emerge, its head held high. Unblinking black eyes, glared straight ahead as it moved. Powerful flippers and tail churned the waters into a long wake behind it. Billy stared at the monster as it steadily paddled upstream and then, suddenly, dove under water again.

He ran all the way to the treatment plant, anxious to share what he had just seen.

"Jimmy, I swear, it was as long as a tractor

trailer. Had grey-green scales and all…A real monster! Just like I seen in school."

"You been drinking too early in the day, again, Billy?" the plant operator said impatiently. He was too busy with the day's tasks to spend time with the town drunk who saw things that probably never were.

"No, Jimmy, I swear. Haven't touched a drop. Yet. But I'd sure like to. That thing was awesomely fierce! Although, it just swam up the river, under the bridge just as calm as could be. Like it belonged there."

Jimmy pulled his wallet out of his back pocket and gave Billy two ten dollar bills. Anything to get him to leave the plant, out of his hair, taking his hallucinations with him.

"Here. Grab your gear and get outta here. This should be enough to cover your, um, expenses for the day. And don't come back here no more. I don't have time for your silliness."

Billy looked at the money in his hand, then scanned Jimmy's face, looking for some semblance of belief in what he was saying. After all, despite being an alcoholic, Billy was the most honest person anyone knew. He'd never unwittingly tell a lie. Jimmy, of all people, should know that. Besides, wasn't Jimmy his friend?

"I…I thank you, Jimmy…" he started to say, "But…"

"But nothing. You hear me? Get outta here. Now!" He turned his back and quickly walked away, wondering if what Billy said he saw was actually what he thought he saw earlier in the sluice. But he wasn't going to relate his own tale again to anyone.

Telling the police, who probably didn't believe him anyway, was one thing.

Sharing his visions with Billy was another.

Billy Bushmill showed up at the Second Street station four hours later, just as Sergeant Henderson was getting ready to go off duty and meet Kelly at the Columbia Hotel for drinks and a light supper. He was characteristically drunk. And while it was obvious he had been drinking most of the afternoon away, he was also vowing never to drink again.

"I'll neber tush anoder drop," he slurred.

Vicki, who had earlier returned from a disappointingly unfulfilled patrol around town with another officer, was at the front desk chatting with Lieutenant Abrams, the officer on duty, when Billy reeled in. She was making a few notations in the police blotter about her visit with Jimmy, flipping through its pages to see if there were any more interesting cases than a big fish in a small murky sluice to be solved.

"There's a monshuh in da riber," Billy said, wiping snot from his nose with the back of his sleeve. Rain dripped from his old, worn Phillies warm-up jacket. He acridly reeked. A little less than a liter of whiskey pouring through his skin.

Henderson wrinkled her nose up at the stench. She closed the blotter and put her pen into a pocket of her blouse.

"Youb haft a do somtink about it," he said, reeling against the large mahogany desk, glaring up at the lieutenant.

"Maybe you ought to sleep it off," Abrams countered.

"No, no, not before..." Billy turned to Vicki. "You believe me, don't you? I tells ya...."

"Tell me what?" She put a handkerchief to her nose as he drew nearer.

"The monshur in da riber."

"A monster, you say?" the policewoman asked, backing away from the skinny, slightly unkempt man crouched before her. *Geez, Louise, he really does stink.* She turned her head to gag into a wad of tissues.

"First thing after he gets booked and into the holding cell is a shower. A cold one," she suggested to Abrams. "At least I'm off duty soon and don't have to be the one to have to deal with the town's worst drunk."

"Gee, thanks, Vicki," Abrams nodded, ignoring Billy.

"Ish was huge!" Billy tried to explain, wanting their full attention, expanding his hands wide to show how big the "monshuh" really was. "At least thirty feet long and four feet wide."

He saw Vicki's stern face turn into a skeptical, then an amused smile and that of the officer at the desk into a cruel, insensitive smirk. "

"Why don't you believe me?" he exclaimed. "Why? I wasn't drunk then. I know what I saw."

"Was it like a big, big fish?" she asked.

"Yesh...and it had...green scales! On its neck. Ish head. All ober its body."

"A monshur, indeed," Lieutenant Abrams snorted, shaking his head. "With green scales Hah! Now, riddle me this. Who would ever believe you?"

"Because I am the town's most honest man," Billy said proudly.

"Now, now, sir," Vicki said, smiling. "He may be a bit inebriated, but being as honest as Billy is, he might just be telling the truth."

MONT CLARE BRIDGE

Charlie McGinty was late getting back to his job as an accountant at the Phoenix Steel Corporation. He had purposely scheduled an eye doctor's appointment in Oaks during his lunch hour, thinking it would be just a quick follow-up to the eye surgery he had had two few weeks ago. A routine check-up was what he thought.

He'd planned to get Chinese take-out at Wong Fu's on his return and be back at his desk in less than an hour. Hour and a half, at the most. But the ophthalmologist had insisted on dilating his pupils so he could get a better look at the repaired retina. Freakishly, Charlie had torn it playing tennis on the Mowere Street courts; slamming his face onto the net cord as he dove for an easy drop shot his opponent had popped over.

It was silly, he admitted later. He should have made the shot and won the point. He should not have tripped. He was more sure-footed than that. But there was a slight buckle in the macadam-composite surface – the courts had been neglected for the past few years or so by the borough's Parks and Recreation Department – and the toe of his worn, fraying Nike had caught on the ripple.

When he fell, he felt the pop. But since there was no pain, he thought nothing of it until he could no longer see the ball over the net. All he saw was a dark patch blotting out vision in his left eye.

Charlie had had emergency surgery at the Wills Eye Center in Philadelphia and, after that, had to see his eye doctor every other day. This Thursday, now that he no longer had to wear the patch, was the first day he was able to get back to work.

It was already past three o'clock when he drove across the county bridge that spanned the Schuylkill River and part of its canal system between Phoenixville and Mont Clare.

It was tax season and the first quarterly report of the year was due in two weeks. The work had piled up in his absence and he was anxious it all wouldn't be completed on time. He had already sat in the waiting room for forty-five minutes waiting for his sight to return. But he couldn't wait any longer. He just couldn't afford to take the extra hour or so for his eyes to revert back to normal. There was work to be done.

So there he was, his vision still a bit blurry, driving slowly across the bridge. And even though it was drizzling rain – hardly any sun – he was wearing his Ray-Ban sunglasses to minimize any glare.

As he slowly drove across the bridge, he glanced to the right to see if the planned lecture and demonstration of the newly restored Lock 60 was well attended. A long-time history buff – especially of local history – he was a member of the Schuylkill Canal Association and had planned on joining his buddy, Banes Monroe, in conducting the tour. He was annoyed that because of work and recovering from his eye injury he would miss it.

He saw a large aluminum canoe being paddled up stream toward the lock. Then, out of the corner of his eye, he was shocked to see what looked like a large serpent's head rising out of the canal waters.

"Oh. My. God!?!" he nearly shouted. "Is that a Nessie? In our river?"

He blinked twice into the rear-view mirror of his creamy white 1975 Buick Skylark to make sure no one was behind him, and then stopped the car in the middle of the bridge.

Not only an avid historian, he was also an amateur photographer and carried a camera with him at all times. Even to work. This day he had a brand new Canon A-1 SLR with a small telephoto lens with him, cradled in its faux-leather case on the passenger seat beside him. Always ready to photograph the unusual, Charlie grabbed the camera and edged his way out of the two-door hatchback, walking as quietly as he could toward the creature.

Like Billy, Charlie had seen many photos of the supposed Loch Ness monster and had often pondered travelling to Scotland to see it for himself. Perhaps he would be the one to actually capture it on film. And now, his chance had come to photograph what as surely its - his? her? - probably younger and definitely smaller cousin.

"Hold still now," he whispered, adjusting the F-stop to maximize clarity and twisting the zoom lens back and forth to get a better look.

Too excited to be afraid, he quickly took at least a dozen shots at various settings and angles, watching through the lens as the beast slowly swiveled its head on its wide elongated neck, as if to gauge the lay of the land and the waters ahead.

Deciding what to do next.

It obviously did not see Charlie taking pictures, but seemed to be startled by the strange constant clicking coming from the bridge above it.

Charlie kept right on shooting as he watch the strange animal roll over on its side, exposing two of its four flipper-like appendages, slapping them onto the water like a child playing patty cake.

"Come on, that's it," the amateur photographer whispered again. "More action."

He willed it to come closer, but his "Nessie"

turned upright again and, with a flick of her/his grey-green head, began to quickly swim upstream to the lock.

Charlie kept right on clicking until the creature slowly disappeared into the mists.

LOCK 60 SKOKIE

The little girl squirmed on the middle thwart and babbled on to herself as her parents navigated their canoe up the stretch of canal from Fitzwater Station. Avid outdoors people, Jake and Mildred Altmeyer tried to spend as much of their free time as they could near or on water.

They had looked forward to this excursion for weeks. Jake had taken the day off from his position as an investment counselor at Phoenixville Bank and Trust. His wife, a stay-at-home mom these past years after Barbara's birth, had just secured a job as an assistant professor at the Valley Forge Christian College. She was to start on Monday.

Their plans made a while ago, they vowed nothing would stop them, not even the drizzling rain that pelted the hoods and backs of their oilskin slickers. Not even a bright, vivacious four-year-old who wiggled and carried on a conversation with herself despite the fact that her parents were not really listening.

They were accustomed to Barbara – Barbie's – constant chatter that sparkled with stories of fairies in the mists, prancing circus horses, and huge birds that twittered outside her bedroom window as she slept.

Her pre-school teacher at the KinderCare center on Gay Street often commented upon her vivid imagination.

"Always about animals, though," the teacher mused during a parent-teacher conference. "She has this fascination with birds that talk, wild horses that she can tame…She once told her friends during recess that she saw pixies in the trees."

"I am amazed you have the patience to even listen to her," Millie commented. "We hear her, but most of what Barbie says seems like nonsense. So, we don't listen." The practical, more down-to-earth type, she shrugged and related that "most of the time I just tend to tune her out."

"Well, you shouldn't," the teacher advised. "Ignore her, I mean. You should really listen. She has some very interesting things to impart. And who's to say they aren't, can't be true?"

Jake smiled as he escorted Millie to their car. "Didn't you find that a bit bizarre? Come now, she has just got to be kidding."

As they passed the large colonial perched upon a hill, overlooking the entrance to the canal, Millie turned and looked back from the bow at her husband.

She pointed up to the house.

"Look. Jake. That's the locktender's house."

"What's a 'tender?" Barbie asked, then continued on with her chatter. She didn't hear her mother's explanation about the keeper of the lock.

"He's the man who years ago took care of the lock. He made the water flow into or out of it to raise and lower the barges so that they can move up or down to the different levels of the canal."

"Do you think they'll even have the re-enactment this afternoon, given the rain?" Jake queried.

"I hope so. We've been planning this for weeks...I'd hate to think us boating in this weather was all for naught."

"Ah, Mil, I thought you liked the rain."

"Only when I'm inside, nice and dry."

"Well, my dear, you'd been fooling me all these years!"

Millie wanly smiled then turned back to the bow and continued paddling.

Obviously, she was the less outdoorsy of the two. But because Jake was so obsessed with all things camping, canoeing, and sailing, she, most times, like today, went along with him, Putting up with rain, cold, the harsh summer sun, insects, and the occasional case of poison ivy.

All because she loved him.

Jake Altmeyer.

Her husband of ten and a half years.

When she graduated in 1969 with a degree in Anthropology from the University of Pennsylvania, she had great plans to join an expedition sponsored by Thor Heyerdahl to Easter Island as part of his on-going studies of the native origins.

She was captivated by his theory that the Philippines had been settled hundreds of years ago by peoples from the Asian mainland who sailed from west to east in nothing more than small outriggers made from bark and bits of cloth. Her thesis had been on the transmutation of ancient Oriental languages to that of the modern day islanders.

"We are thrilled," Dr. Heyerdahl said in a letter confirming her acceptance, "to have you on board as an integral part of the team." He, of course, won't be part of the trip. He was already travelling between Morocco and Bolivia overseeing the construction of the Ra, a boat constructed entirely of papyrus that he intended to sail across the Atlantic Ocean.

It really didn't matter. Fresh out of graduate school, Millie had been excited even to be recognized by the famed explorer, let alone be welcomed as part of what would have been her first expedition.

But her plans were disrupted the weekend before she was to fly to Shanghai.

Jake really didn't want to go to the party. He had had his fill of drinking and carousing and protesting in college. He had returned to his hometown and settled in nicely at the local bank where his father had been one of the vice presidents. He was used to counseling others on where to put their money while investing his own during the week and spending his weekends on solitary camping trips in the various parks and camp sites in Chester and Montgomery counties.

But his former roommate from Columbia University, his new bride, and two other couples were passing through town on their way to Florida. Doug had begged for him to join them for dinner.

"Hey, you're not married, pal," he said to Jake when he called. "You really have nothing to do...Right? Why not just come along?"

"I am not one for crowds, remember? Besides I do have plans."

"What? Playing with Woody Woodpecker in the forest? Or reading the latest accounting best seller?

"Knock it off, Doug. As much as I'd like to see you..."

"Then come. There's only six of us. We'll have a few drinks, dinner....Fun!"

Which was the last thing he wanted to have that

evening.

Reluctantly, however, feeling very much like a fifth, er, seventh wheel, he agreed to meet them on the front porch of the Columbia Hotel where they were staying. Doug suggested they decide where to go next after they had dined.

Mildred's father was proud as a peacock of his daughter.

"A major expedition - her first - right out of graduate school. Mmm-mmm. Ain't that something?" he bragged for days to his customers who came into his upholstery shop nestled on the corner of Gay Street and Prospect Avenue.

He had every reason to.

Hundreds of yards of hand-sewn brocades, damasks, twill cottons, and the occasional denim had gone into paying for her college education. Now he was about to see all of his – and her – hard work come to fruition.

"C'est un cause célèbre," he said in his native French. "I am taking you and the family to dinner! Chez La Columbia!"

Their entrees had just been served when the raucous party of seven in the barroom was seated at the table next to them. Mildred was surprised to see the tall, handsome young man wearing what looked like a hand-tailored sport coat and an open necked Oxford button-down shirt, obviously single, join the three couples.

Crossing the room between crisp white linen tablecloths and shiny silver serving trays and carts, he espied her, too. A young woman with long brunette hair carefully twisted into a bun at the nape of her neck. Strikingly limpid blue eyes.

Obviously dining out with her parents and two brothers. With her family.

Obviously single.

He managed to secure the seat next to her.

He smiled.

She shyly smiled back, and then initiated a conversation.

When they discovered they had both attended Phoenixville High – Go Phantoms! – only two years apart, they mused together why they hadn't met sooner. Then they traded jokes and stories about former classmates and wizened teachers.

It was all it took.

They were married four months later at St. Peter's Episcopal Church and began their life together in a two-bedroom Pickering Run apartment. Later they would move to a large Victorian in the 100 block of 2nd Avenue with large side and back yards and a huge shed where Jake could store his sundry camping equipment.

Millie never made it on her first expedition.

Although she did often quip with her dry, droll sense of humor that living with her husband was all the adventure she needed.

As their canoe approached the wooden dock that paralleled the bank at the foot of the lock, a small group of people wound their way down the path from the house. A few of the men were dressed in late 1880s garb – loose-fitting trousers, blue denim shirts, thick-soled hobnail boots – apparently to mimic those who plied their barges filled with coal from the Reading Mines on the Schuylkill Navigation System to the factories in Philadelphia.

Millie and Jake tied up their small craft behind one of the barges that would be used for the 3:30 demonstration of how a canal lock worked.

Barbie clambered out of the canoe and raced ahead of her parents. She jostled her way into the small gathering on the walkway over the lock to hear a member of the canal association dedicated to its preservation relate a little bit of history.

The lock and the canal were built in the early 1800s by Irish immigrants who had fled to America from one of the first great potato famines, seeking a better, richer life.

They were employed by the hundreds by the Schuylkill Navigation Company, incorporated in 1815 to make the shallow Schuylkill River navigable for the many barges that would carry the largess of resources from the inner parts of Pennsylvania. Anthracite coal, flour, flax, and a host of many manufactured goods were among the more popular items ferried downstream to Philadelphia and smaller communities along the way.

It took ten years to construct the 108-mile canal system, linking the Port Carbon coal fields with what was quickly becoming the third largest and second most profitable city in the eastern United States. With Herculean efforts, the Irishmen completed the first man-made canal system in May of 1825, months ahead of schedule.

They were rewarded for their sunup to sundown back-breaking efforts with fifty cents a day, a meager ration of whiskey, and the prospect of dying an early death with cholera or malaria. But they repaid their employers with nightly rounds of violence, heavy drinking, armed conflicts, and labor riots.

The Irish workers were, nonetheless, dedicated and built the canal as well as Lock 60, one of the few working ones still remaining on the Schuylkill River today.

Banes Munroe, the guide, concluded his short lecture. Then he turned and indicated a long, low flat scow tied to the river bank.

"Now, if you all would join me on the barge over there, we'll proceed with the reenactment."

Barbie was fascinated, and, for once, quiet, as she watched from the back of the barge the man pretending to be the 'tender hand crank open the huge steel doors of the lock.

"We don't have any mules to pull us through," Banes explained, "so we just gotta improvise. He pulled a rip cord to start up the 15HP Evinrude outboard motor attached to one corner of the stern. "Just enough horse, er ass power to get us up into the lock and then upstream," he quipped.

Millie frowned at the derogatory term for a pack animal, pointing to her daughter.

"Er, sorry, I meant...mule power. Sorry, M'am," he whispered, tipping the brim of his woolen fisherman's cap. "So very sorry."

He guided the gas-powered barge into the lock, cut off the motor, and then signaled for one of the enactors standing near the lock to crank the doors closed. When he was sure they were sealed, he started up the engine again and slowly steered the barge though the lock to its upstream doors. The enactor walked alongside on the towpath.

Once in position, Banes signaled for the enactor to crank open the sluices that fed the lock with water. The lock ever so slowly filled up; ever so slowly raising the barge, with its passengers and crew, up to the level of the river above the dam.

"This process is done in reverse as a barge moves downstream," Banes explained to the small cadre of passengers now huddled in the bow. "Normally, of course, it would be empty, having delivered its goods to Philadelphia. Now...let me explain..."

But just as Banes began yet another segment of the Lock's history, Barbie, who had been assiduously watching the water rise up the walls of the lock, began jumping up and down, exclaiming and pointing with delight.

"There's a fairy lake dragon. Look, Mommy, a real live fairy lake dragon!" tugging at her mother's slicker sleeve. "Right beside us!"

Millie looked toward where her daughter was pointing and watched through the after-rain mist as a large shadow nested alongside the barge. She wasn't sure what she was seeing and reached to clasp Jake's hand.

"Do you see that?"

"More importantly, does Mr. Munroe see it?"

Barbie, in her excitement, began once again to babble about "the fairy dragon."

"His name is Skokie. Hi, Skokie!" she called, waving frantically to get its attention. "Hi, it's me, Barbie. Hey, Skokie, what are you doing here in the lock with us?" she cried as he, it, "Skokie" – as if river monsters even had a name – rolled over onto its side and blinked.

"Look, Mommy, he winked at me."

"It's just a shadow, honey. Isn't it, Jake?"

"Shadows don't wink, Barbie," he said, holding his wife close. "Er, um, Mr. Munroe...Banes, I think you ought to see this."

Banes Monroe scrambled over to the side of the barge and peered overboard. He wasn't sure what he was seeing, either. But apparently the something was more than a mere shadow and, whatever it was, had accompanied them into the lock and was now patiently waiting for the water to rise and the upstream doors to open so that it could continue its journey.

Barbie leaned further over the side of the barge, chattering away at her new-found friend floating peacefully in the water alongside the barge. Just as if he – she? – knew what was to happen next.

With one eye on the suspicious "shadow" and the other in the re-enactor on shore, Banes counted the minutes out loud until the water level in the lock had reached the level of the river.

"Now!" he shouted, signaling for the doors to be cranked open.

As Banes started up the small Evinrude again to exit the lock, the waters alongside its walls began to boil. The huge, 20-foot shadow rose up through the water; what looked a head almost breaking the surface. Millie thought she saw a fin and blinked three times to wipe the image from her mind.

"Skokie" swam out of the lock into the canal. A giant serpent's head mounted on a barreled neck appeared as the creature leapt up out of the water, seemingly, literally, jumping for joy.

Or so Barbie had stated, in a clear, crisp, high voice, clapping her hands. Then, in a rare, unlike-their-daughter countenance, she seriously queried her parents.

"What is it, Mommy? Daddy? What do you really think it is?"

Millie wasn't sure what she saw. And she had no explanations for her inquisitive child.

Just as they were about to navigate up the canal

parallel to the river, "Skokie" quickly swam ahead, He, she, it was now just above the dam that had earlier that morning proved an almost formidable obstacle.

The shadow once again thrashed about and then quickly swam upstream to the center of the river where it once again reared up. Its seemingly ugly head perched high on top of a long, sinewy thick, grey-scaled neck.

Millie tried to remember what she had learned in her zoological class at the University of Pennsylvania.

"A 'Nessie'. A smaller one, of course, otherwise it wouldn't fit in the Schuylkill. But still, a Nessie all the same," she calmly stated, not quite sure if Barbie had actually seen anything. After all, she was a very imaginative child. Or was it her own imagination playing mirage tricks in the distant late afternoon mists above the lock?

Jake quick grabbed his camera from his oversized fanny pack, aimed and took what later turned out to be nothing more than large dark blotches against the lighter shadows of spritzing rain. Even when he tried to enlarge them later, the photos showed nothing but a blurred outline of what they could only suppose could be a large tree limb that had fallen from a dead sycamore into the waters and had floated end up out into the middle of the river.

"What is that, Mommy?" Barbie insistently asked

again. "Is it the fairy dragon?"

"No, dear." She smiled. "I think it might be a cousin of, um...the Loch Ness Monster. You know, the big creature that lives in the lake in Scotland?"

Barbie shook her head. She had no idea what her mother was talking about. To her, it was a large sea horse, like in the movie. All she wanted to do was to reach out and touch its green scales, sooth its furrowed brow, talk to it in fairy dragon nickers and neighs.

And tell her teacher about it in school. She knew that even though no one else did, Miss Carson would believe her

Banes Monroe wasn't sure what he was seeing, either. He heard about the monster sightings in Scotland, but being a very practical man, assumed the legend was nothing but a hoax to attract tourists. If it were true, as Mrs. Altmeyer said, the shadow swimming up the canal was a smaller version of "Nessie", who was he to argue against the business that would result from visitors flocking to Phoenixville to see it?

He watched as Millie and Jake listen closely to their daughter's babbling.

"Fairy dragon in the water," she started to chant. "See it winking. Watch it swimming."

He looked again and saw the head and neck rising

through the mists, as clearly as could be seen on such a dismal day.

"Maybe we should call someone," Jake Altmeyer suggested to no on in particular. "Have them come out and take a look."

"What ever it is, it's travelling too fast upriver," Banes Monroe said. "It would be long gone by the time the police got here."

Millie pressed Barbie's head into her stomach, hiding her face and covering her ears.

"That would only scare my child," she said. "I'll call Nancy Crockett at *The Evening Phoenix* when we get home"

Little did they know that the savvy, silvery grey-haired newspaper editor had already begun compiling a manila folder full of phone messages and notes about various sightings of the strange monster swimming in the river.

TOPPER REILLY'S COW

Built in the early 1890s, the Columbia Hotel on Bridge Street was reputed to be one of the more elegant establishments in the Phoenixville area. It not only accommodated overnight guests, but its French Country Room restaurant was renowned for its elegant ambiance, serving open-flame grilled steaks and fresh seafood.

The barroom, with its array of exotic as well as common potent potables, sported a large dark cherry bar with a thick, marble top. Intricate figures and flowers were carved into its front and sides. Behind it hung a large mirror with two semi-nude odalisques, hand-painted in pastels. The more salient parts tastefully obscured by a vast array of bottles and decanters on three tiers of glass shelves

Columbia Hotel's front porch, garnished with a green and white striped awning and an "1890 Gaslight" sign over the facade, was, for close to ninety years, a favorite meeting place. A starting-off point for many business as well as personal appointments and endeavors.

Shortly after six o'clock that evening, Topper Reilly stormed into the hotel's barroom. Shaking rain off his oil-skin slicker in the lobby, he pushed his short, pudgy frame through the double saloon slatted doors and bellowed for his usual Gordon's double dry martini. Then he settled himself in the booth solely dedicated for his use. An aging sot who, by virtue of his seniority and a chronic addiction to Gordon's, he had long ago claimed this entitlement.

Like Vicki Henderson, Topper Reilly was a transplant. He had owned a forty-acre farm, inherited from his great-uncle in King of Prussia, but wasn't that interested in agriculture. When a contractor contacted him to buy the land to erect what had become the King of Prussia Plaza, he quickly signed the paperwork and moved further northeast and purchased five acres bordering Township Line Road and Route 23. There he built his own mini-mall with his now famous Tarrytowne Hardware Store and Emporium.

While he was a native of the area, Topper wasn't from Phoenixville itself. To the local born and bred residents he was not nor would be considered a "true" son of historic Victorian steel town. Even though he was now a borough councilman and wielded a lot of political weight and influence he was, in fact, often considered by many of the native locals an interloper, an intruder, an outsider.

Phoenixville's "true" natives were natural snobs,

proud of their town.

Yet...

No one seated in the room or standing at the long bar questioned the authority of the short, squat, pudgy man. If anyone opposed him, he'd figure out a way to raise his taxes or refuse him service in his store. Just about everyone gave him a silent, respectfully wide berth in his presence; but often talked and laughed about him behind his back.

"Good goddamn!" he hollered to no one in particular. "Let me tell you what happened to me today!" Everyone was more interested in their own conversation over the all-you-can-eat buffet dinner served on Thursday nights, not wishing the enjoyment of their evening meal ruined by Topper's constantly surly, negative commentaries about everything and everybody. Yet, they all turned their heads toward him to hear what he had to say.

"You all know about that Guernsey cow I got to provide my baby granddaughter's daily milk?" he asked as he crossed to his booth table and sat down.

Two men closest to him nodded over their pints of pale ale, wishing he would just go away. Leave them alone. Who cared about his darn cow, anyway?

"Well, it got itself missing this afternoon! And I'm looking for the creep who stole it!"

When his martini was served by the timid

bartender, he swilled it down in one gulp. "Bring me another, twerp!"

"Why he'd even get a cow in the first place," one of the ale drinkers whispered to his buddy, "when Flynn provides most of the milk around here? Seems to me a waste of time and money."

"I heard that, ya creep!" Reilly stood up and tried to loom over their table. At less than five feet four inches, his head barely reached over the shoulders of the tall, sitting men. "I got me the cow 'cause I can guarantee the milk is fresh. Somethin' O'Rourke sometimes can't do."

"What are you saying, Topper? Flynn's milk...is?"

"Sours just as soon as it leaves the tit of his old cows. Even worse when his nervous twit of a wife doesn't get it pasteurized in time. Think I'd give that to my new grandbaby, ya idjit!?! She's colicky enough as it is..."

"Sorry, Topper. Don't take offense," the ale drinker, whose name was Frank Webber, retorted. "My kids drink the milk Flynn and his family supply to Forresta's and they're fine..."

"Ah, shut your trap, Frank," Reilly said and ordered yet a third double-dry martini.

As the exchange continued, all conversation in the barroom as well as in the downstairs dinning area stopped. It was so quiet, you could hear the side of beef roasting on a spit in the back kitchen.

"So, getting back to my missing cow..." Reilly turned to others in the bar and glared at them, not quite looking into their faces. Reilly was never one to look anyone in the eye. "If any of you all know what happened to it, you'd be obliged to tell me. 'Cause I am hopping, stinking mad."

Frank's buddy, who really didn't care one way or the other, asked Reilly to continue his story.

"Around dawn I hear the damn cow bawling in the makeshift shed we put up in the backyard for it. But when I got outta bed and went out the back door, all I could find was a huge deep groove in the soil leading down to the river. And the cow was gone."

"Now why would anybody want to steal your Ol' Bossy?" the bartender asked quietly when he returned with the rich, fusty old man's second and third drinks.

"That's what I said. I hope when they catch them I get a chance to wield my authority around here. Get 'em treated like they did cow thieves in the old west. Hang 'em high!" He took a large slurp of a martini. "Until then," he said. "Until the stink'n perp comes forward or the police catch him – one way or t'other – the thirty percent off sale at my store is hereby cancelled."

Kelly, of course, was there that night, sipping her own usual double-dry martini. She and Vicki Henderson, now finally off-duty, were already sitting at the bar trading small talk when Reilly first barreled in, shouting about his missing cow.

O'Rourke strolled in a half-hour or so later after he had finished his milk deliveries to have a quick drink. He was heading home for supper and was dreading having to tell his dear Kat what had happened that morning to their geese. He thought a two-finger tumbler of rye whiskey would bring him a bit of courage.

When he heard O'Reilly continue to boast over and over about the "large groove" in his backyard, his dander was fired up and he and Reilly began shouting at each other, trading their tales of what had happened, what they had – or hadn't – seen that day. What, who they thought the thief was.

"I tell you, it was a damn river monster," O'Rourke said, quoting what Sergeant Henderson had said to him that morning at the police station. He nodded over to her sitting at the bar, a shy grin on his face as if to ask, "Am I right?"

Kelly watched Vicki imperceptibly nod as she took another sip of her drink. "What was that all about?"

the reporter asked herself. Something is going on here, she realized. But she wasn't sure exactly what it was.

She sat quietly, wishing she had opted to have a quiet dinner at home and then go see *The Boys of Company C* currently playing at the Colonial Theater. She was an ardent fan of Bette Midler and tried not to miss any of her movies. Yet, here she was, sitting at the large bar, perplexed at Vicki, listening to the two men arguing.

Each one trying to top the other.

"Ah, you're full of hockey-puck doo-doo," Topper smirked. Even if he was a crude, coarse old man, he was sometimes careful to watch his language around "the ladies". "Weren't no monster. Someone with a snow sledge or a large aluminum canoe, that's who got my cow. Someone who needs to add a young milker to his herd."

"What?! Are you accusing me of stealing your cow?"

"I didn't say that, O'Rourke. You just did..."

"Why you son of a..." Flynn stopped him in mid-sentence. There was no use arguing with the man. He, himself, knew the truth, and the owner of Tarrytowne Hardware was just a small, fat blowhard who was always vying for attention.

O'Rourke quickly downed the rest of his drink,

tired from his long day and of Topper's ranting about his cow being stolen. He left a ten dollar bill on the marble top of the bar and, without saying good-bye, silently walked out of the room.

The way he was feeling, he decided not to tell dear Kat anything about the geese until he was in a better mood.

When Billy Bushmill came in later that evening, he seemed cold sober, although he had drank most of the afternoon away. After his visit to the police that afternoon, he had gone to his mother's apartment where he napped and showered. He was now dressed in clean, neatly pressed clothes, looking as dapper as he could possibly be.

The Columbia's usual Thursday night crowd was surprised not only at his appearance, but was astounded when he approached the bar and ordered from the timid bartender a ginger ale over ice with a lime twist instead of his usual triple fingers of Irish whisky.

Standing loosely confident, leaning against the bar, his cold drink in hand, he started to relate his own story about what he had seen earlier that afternoon from the Pawlings Road Bridge.

Kelly once again took out her steno pad and started to take notes.

"Listen to them," Vicki, whispered into her second

double-shot-of-vodka Bloody Mary. A drop of tomato juice glistened on her upper lip. "Nothing but a big fish story."

"But you said this morning when O'Rourke came in..."

"True, I did suggest it," Vicki chuckled, munching on the celery stalk garnish. "In jest, my friend..."

"But what about Billy Bushmill? He claims to have seen it, too..."

"And you believe that drunk?"

"Sure. And all those unexplained incidences. Mr. O'Rourke's geese. Reilly's cow. The fisherman's story," she continued, explaining the anonymous phone call she had received in the newsroom. "And the sightings...Different times, in different places, right? They can't all be coincidental." Kelly took another sip of her drink, savoring the tart taste of the Plymouth gin, trying to quell her suspicions.

"It was huge," Billy was saying to his rapt audience. "Swimming right up the river, under the bridge, large, green-scaled head on a long, sinewy neck held high above the water, proud as could be, as if it owned the river. Like it was its own private swimming pool."

Kelly quickly copied down his words in her modified journalistic shorthand. She would decipher it later the next day when she enfolded them into her article.

"See?" she nudged her friend. "He's the most honest man in town, Vicki. He's adamant about seeing the green-scaled head, too. Just like the guy I spoke to. Different times, different places. Same river. That proves it just has to be true."

"Could be. But, don't believe everything you hear or see, Kelly."

She took another thoughtful sip of her Bloody Mary.

"Phoenixville," she mused, "is well known for its practical jokes."

THE NEXT DAY

Kelly was relentless in her pursuit of a story. Once she had a nibble of a lead, she'd gnaw on it until it grew. First came the appetizing opening paragraph – the who, what, when, where, and how. It had to be a grabber. Then came the nuts and bolts, the main ingredients of the entrée. She would interview people unceasingly, digging deeper and deeper, stirring and folding whatever she had uncovered into the article until it was as close to a full five-course meal as she could get it.

Of course, the topper, the desert, was one of her infamous tag lines, often written with a dash of sugary humor.

Tongue-in-cheek.

It was no different with her story about the Schuylkill River Monster.

After what she had heard last night in the barroom of the Columbia Hotel, she was convinced some, most, if not all of it was true. With all the various "confirmed" sightings, coupled with the mysteriously slaughter of local livestock, what was lurking in and creeping out of the shadows of the waters around Phoenixville just had to be what

Sergeant Henderson had suggested and what Flynn O'Rourke, the unknown fisherman, and Billy Bushmill had said it was.

A river monster.

With next to no sleep, Kelly left her one-bedroom flat over Seacrist's Stationary just after sunrise that morning and nearly ran the three-quarters of a block to the Phoenix Publishing Company building where the editorial offices of *The Evening Phoenix* were housed. Her first task was to convince Nancy Crockett, the managing editor, of the validity of her proposed story.

It wasn't like Kelly to gush. She was nearly thirty-one, a seasoned reporter who had once somberly worked for *The New York Times*, writing obituaries, setting her sights on a more glamorous, less drearily depressing spot on the features desk. She had hopes of working alongside a former college classmate and friend, Josey McIvers, who concentrated on tennis features, interviews of the professionals, and color coverage sidebars of the majors. The more "choice" assignments.

When Kelly was told she'd be working on what Josey termed "the dregs" – local interest in and around the Big Apple suburbs – she decided it might be better to be a big fish in a small pond than a tadpole floundering in the big ocean of *The New York*

Times. She took the position anyway, biding her time.

Even while her assignments were dull and often boring, Kelly took it all in her stride, assiduously honing her craft until one of her more prominent bylined stories hit the wires of the Associated Press.

Nancy had been impressed with Kelly's coverage of the 1976 Bicentennial Celebration held in Center City, in and around Philadelphia's famed Independence Hall. Hoards of tourists dressed as colonialists; President Johnson's failed attempt to strike a chord on the cracked Liberty Bell; the re-enactment of the signing of the Declaration of Independence; the sprinklings of Benjamin Franklin quotes throughout. The editor slotted it onto the front page of *The Evening Phoenix*, convinced that it was good enough to earn Kelly a request to "come be an integral part of our staff".

Fed up with playing second fiddle, Kelly left what could have eventually been a prestigious career to wend her own way as a star reporter for a little known suburban newspaper that served a small, obscure community hidden in the recessed hills of eastern Pennsylvania.

That was just over a year ago.

And now, after months of covering local fires, petty-larceny arrests, and seemingly meaningless local elections, this was her big chance. Who knows?

If Nancy agreed, and the article was good enough, it might even make it to the Associated Press with a national byline. Her name.

The tall, red-headed editor looked up from the article she was redacting as Kelly eagerly approached. The aging, seasoned newspaper woman was an early-riser, too, often strolling into the dark offices of the paper before dawn to get "crackin' on the day's news."

"I think I have a whopper of a story, boss." Kelly tried to contain her excitement behind a façade of seriousness.

"Let me guess," Nancy smiled at the petite, curly-haired brunette. "It's about the sightings in the river yesterday."

"Yeah, how did you know?" Kelly's blue eyes danced in anticipation of being allowed to continue to work on the story.

"We got phone calls all afternoon. Here, you might want to use this."

She handed the eager features reporter the manila folder with ten or more phone messages along with a few cryptic notes about the supposed creature that looked like the Loch Ness Monster swimming in the waters of the Schuylkill River around Black Rock Dam and Lock 60. Along with the pink slips was an old clipping from *The New York Times* about five sightings of the Loch Ness Monster from 1960 through 1973.

"For background color," Nancy explained with a chuckle. "You might want to include it in your story. Give it a little bit of authenticity."

"Sure..." Kelly knitted her brow. "Er, does this mean I can go with it?"

"Yes, I think so. It would make an interesting piece for tomorrow's paper, don't you think? Especially given the date..." The editor smiled again, and then nodded. "Make sure you follow up on those phone leads...to collaborate what you write."

Shaking her head slightly in amusement, she waved a slender, deeply tanned hand in the air over her head, dismissing Kelly to her work.

Although reports of an aquatic beast living in Loch Ness in the Scottish Highlands had been related for more than 1,500 years, the article stated, the first "legitimate" sighting of the Loch Ness Monster was on May 2, 1933. *The Inverness Courier* reported that a local couple had seen "an enormous animal rolling and plunging on the surface" and had attempted to take its picture. What the photograph depicted was a large serpent's neck on top of a thick, elongated neck rising up out of the waters from an oblong, sperm whale-like torso.

According to reputed scholars, the story of the "monster" dates back to 500 A.D. when local Picts carved a strange aquatic creature into standing stones near Loch Ness. The earliest written reference to a monster in Loch Ness is Saint Columba's 7th-century biography by Adomnan. The saint was the Irish missionary who introduced Christianity to Scotland.

In 565, according to the biographer, Columba was on his way to visit the king of the northern Picts near Inverness. Hearing about a beast that had been killing people in the lake, he stopped at Loch Ness, where he saw a monster about to attack another man. Confronting the monster, Columba intervened by diving into the water, invoking the name of God, making the Sign of the Cross, and commanding the creature to "go back into the deep with all speed." The monster retreated and never killed another man.

"Nessie", as the monster has been dubbed, had lain low, as it were, for more than 1,400 years until the couple spied her as they stood on the loch's shore near the village of Drumnadrochit. She sparked fervor for sightings and the then newly-formed Loch Ness Monster Investigation Team began vigilantly watching the waters of the 800-foot deep, 23-mile long lake. Subsequent operations and expeditions have revealed a large, humpbacked aquatic animal lurking in the shadow surface, but clear, precise, definitive photographs have yet to be taken.

Thought to be of the phylum and class cryptoid kelpielatus, she has been known to make brief appearances all along the loch's shore. Similar, but smaller creatures believed to be members of the same species have been sighted in lakes and deep rivers all across Europe and parts of North America.

While carnivorous, they often eschew beef and are reputed to subsist on fish, water fowl, and indigenous vegetation.

"Why, it's just like the fisherman and Billy Bushmill described it," Kelly said, re-reading the sheet of paper. "But our monster is smaller, much smaller...I wonder if she is one of Nessie's cousins?" She pondered for a while, and then said, "Of course. It just had to be."

Deciding to include portions of the article into her own, Kelly highlighted a few more sections and then carefully put it back into the folder.

Settled back at her desk, Kelly sorted the phone messages by time received, noting the names of each of the callers. Some she knew from doing previous stories; others were vaguely familiar; still others were total unknowns. On a blank 8.5x11 leaf of newsprint, she drew a chart, carefully plotting times and, when supplied, where the monster was seen. Then she photocopied a map of Phoenixville and placed dots corresponding to the chart where the sightings and incidences were.

When she saw the message from Millie Altmeyer about her daughter's claim to see "Skokie" in Lock 60 and then "dancing in the waters above the dame" around 3:45 p.m., she placed it in front of her telephone and dialed the number.

'I don't think I can allow that," Millie tried to explain when Kelly requested an interview with Barbie. She was annoyed that the reporter had the very nerve intruding on their privacy so early in the morning. "It would be too devastating for her. She is too traumatized as it is."

"Well, you did call the paper last evening," Kelly countered. "Might I use what you told the night editor in my article?" Kelly waited for an answer, then quickly added, "Anonymously, of course."

Millie put the phone down on the kitchen counter and walked into the family room to ask Jake his opinion. She didn't want Kelly to hear their conversation. All Kelly could hear over the line was the faint ticking of a clock.

"Hello," she said, "Hello?" Anybody there?"

When Millie finally got back on the line three minutes later, she said, "Yes, you may. But only if it is anonymous. No one must know it was our daughter."

"Guar-run-teed!" Kelly smiled. "Thank you."

When Kelly hung up the phone, Nancy popped her head out of her office and told the reporter she had a visitor in the outer lobby.

"Did he ask for me? Personally?" She was hoping that handsome cohort of Vicki's she had met the night before on the all-you-can-eat buffet line would stop by for coffee on his way to the police station.

"No, but I think you're the one he should be talking to."

Charlie McGinty had taken a total of twenty-five pictures. Out of ten or so relatively good ones, only five showed any promise. The rest had been blurry shots through the rain or ruined when he uncharacteristically had impatiently ripped the roll out of the camera. Of the five, two showed distinct shapes; definitely identifiable as a "monster in the water". One of a head, neck, and the upper torso. The second of it on its side, slapping the water with two flippers as Charlie's beast rolled and cavorted before heading upstream.

"These are definite proof," Kelly Pearce had smiled when he showed her the two copies each of the best monster photographs he had brought. "Where did you take these?"

Charlie related all that he had seen standing in the rain on the Mont Clare Bridge that previous afternoon as the reporter made a notation on what would finally become her "official" Map of Sightings and Incidences.

"Well, that makes sense," she stated, indicating the highlighted lines she had drawn to indicate the monster's path. Yellow for going downstream; light blue for swimming back up. "So far, it starts here in Mingo, at O'Rourke's Dairy. If, indeed, it was what got the geese. Then, above Black Rock Dam. Spotted by a fisherman."

"You mean, I am not the only one who saw it?' Charlie asked disappointedly. He had thought he'd be the only one. Become the one person in town who had espied a Loch Ness Monster – or a smaller version thereof – in the waters of their famed river.

"Oh, no!" Kelly exclaimed when she saw Charlie's crestfallen look. She frowned, "I'm sorry …" Then smiled, "But…you were the only one with enough foresight to take pictures."

Charlie's face, pallid by years working the steel

company's books under harsh fluorescent lights, lit up again.

"I'm the only one to take pictures."

"And good ones at that," Kelly added, giving him a broad grin of encouragement.

Charlie smiled back and then looked down at her chart.

'So, show me where my Nessie went."

"Well. She swam all the way down the river to the treatment plant."

"Without being seen?" Charlie asked.

"Apparently. Most of the sightings were when it was heading up the river. After Jimmy, then Billy, you later that afternoon...And then in the lock by little Barbie Altmeyer."

"The banker's daughter?"

"Yes, according to her mother."

"And you believe them? Her? A little girl?"

"Of course. Even with their vivid imaginations, I think children are much more candid and truthful than adults. Yes, with all these sightings, I believe them all." She paused. "But you're the one who took its picture. Don't you believe in what you shot?"

"Sure do," Charlie said. "That's a monster in the river...Must be true."

"Must be. Um, can I use these? We'll pay you, of course. Put your name under the captions..."

"That'd be swell."

At least, he thought proudly, leaving the Phoenix Publishing Co. building to drive his Skylark to work.

"Even if I weren't the only person to see it, I was the first to take the official pictures."

Kelly carefully carried the photographs back to her desk.

"What a coup," she chuckled out loud. "Actual photographs of the thing. Just wait until I show these to Vicki."

But, before she could do that, she had other tasks to attend to.

The first one was to sort the messages in what she thought would be the order of importance and probability, comparing them with the notes she had taken yesterday evening in the barroom and earlier this morning from the police blotter entries. She decided the stories of Flynn O'Rourke and Topper Reilly would comprise the meat of her story. After all, they were two of the more prominent citizens of Phoenixville. And the most reliable.

She decided to interview O'Rourke first, since he was the first to surmise the killer of his geese wasn't human, but much more than a hungry fox or a rabid dog. Much more. She thought it best to talk to him in person.

Without bothering to call him, she stuffed pens and an extra steno pad – just in case she needed it – into her already crammed-full messenger bag, hastily left the office without saying where she was going, and hopped into her bright yellow Karmen Ghia convertible.

It was a short five-minute drive up Second Avenue along the western shore of the Schuylkill to O'Rourke's Dairy.

As she drove, enjoying the humming of the four-cylinder German engine behind her and the feel of manually shifting gears as she revved the gas and took the sinuous turns of Second Avenue along the river at a fast clip, she began outlining her front-page article in her mind.

She pictured the large, bold headline with her name underneath.

UNEXPLAINED EVENTS PUZZLE POLICE
ACE REPORTER SOLVES THE CRIMES
KELLY PEARCE
STAFF REPORTER

O'Rourke

Flynn O'Rourke was a native of Phoenixville, a member of one of the most respected and, despite its history, respectable families in the area.

He had been born on his parent's dairy farm in Mingo, which he inherited and, in 1978, still ran. He was proud of his Irish ancestry and his family's accomplishments. Pleased as punch every day about how far they had come from a dirt-poor farm in eastern Ireland to being some of the more prominent residents of Phoenixville.

Flynn's great-grandfather, for example was one of the hundreds of Irish immigrants who had drudged and dredged and dug to build the Schuylkill canal system, Unlike many of the other workers, he had somehow managed to save most of his meager wages and, after Lock 60 was finally finished, purchase a forty-acre plot of land along the river in a lower section of Mingo that was considered part of Phoenixville proper.

He began his dairy herd with four cows and a bull purchased at auction in nearby Kimberton and had herded the cows home up Rapps Dam Road, across Mowere, and the length of Township Line Road. He then crossed farmland to the west shore of the river and forded a narrow, shallow part of it to his acreage below Mingo. It took the better part of a day, stopping traffic on the major routes, and making friends along the way. The bull he had carted by two of the auctioneer's assistants; part of the total sale price for the cattle.

Gallegan O'Rourke had thus earned his reputation as a stubborn, yet resourceful, albeit friendly man. His herd grew to thirty head. He added prime laying hens, a rooster, and a gaggle of geese. He hired three farm workers and their wives, adept on making butter and cheese. And as the farm grew, O'Rourke's Dairy became the number one producer and supplier of dairy and poultry products in the area. When he died at 87 he was, by reckoning in those days, a wealthy man.

The farm was passed on to Patrick O'Rourke, Gillie's second son, who was at the time one of the strictest, most stern-faced teachers in the eight-sided schoolhouse. An instructor of basic reading, writing, and arithmetic, he had a reputation for being a strict disciplinarian. Known as "Paddy" because of his Irish brogue, he had an irate temper and an array of sticks of varying thicknesses he did not hesitate to use when a young boy didn't recite his lessons correctly or questioned his authority.

Paddy was also one of the town imbibers and was famous for picking fights with the fathers of his charges when they didn't agree with his methods of education. When his own father died, he instantly quit his teaching post, much to the relief of his students and their parents, and took over the farm,

He was set in earnest to double the size of his wealth and triple the size of the herd.

In time, Paddy had made enough to replace the long, low one story two-room log cabin with a large, three story brick farmhouse. Tall colonnades rose in front of a massive veranda, supporting a second-floor screened-in sleeping porch. He painted the house bright yellow and erected ornate wrought-iron fencing – custom-made at the Phoenix Iron Works – around it to keep his free-range chickens from pecking on and messing up the well-tended lawns.

While it was from Gallegan that Flynn had acquired his droll sense of humor and his astute business acumen, he inherited Paddy's fierce anger, which, unlike his grandfather, he tried very hard to keep it at bay. Flynn had also inherited his affection for fine whiskey from his father, Gallegan the Second – Paddy's only son and, besides the land and a barely neglected plantation house, very little else.

In the middle of the Great Depression of the 1930s, Gillie had lost half the herd, slaughtered a bull to sell the meat and feed himself and wife, and through neglect had let most of the chickens die out. He nearly lost the rest shooting craps behind the old Foundry building playing with five of the more burly ironworkers.

But one afternoon, betting everything he had, including the farm and the ten dollars he had left remaining in his pocket, he managed, against all odds, to roll a lucky seven and, to his amazement, clean up.

Gillie had enough to restock the farm, buy a new bull, and plow and reseed ten acres of corn and barley. Which was, for all intents and purposes, his biggest dream. To prove to himself, his pregnant wife, and to his dead father that he was every inch the kind of men that Gallegan the First and Patrick were. At least that was his plan.

But, besides being an incompetent businessman, a lazy farmer, and a dreamer, Gallegan the Second also liked whiskey, wagering on the ponies, and women.

In that order.

In mid-afternoon of May 1, 1935, he ambled slightly tipsy into the back room of a dusky bar on Emmett Street, diagonally across from St. Mary's Cemetery where his father was buried. Betting of any sort was illegal in Chester County, except at the Philadelphia race tracks. But Gillie was too poor, too busy to take the time to drive to Bensalem or down to

Brandywine Park in Delaware for the trotters. Besides, with the depression going on, there was barely any money for gas for his truck, a beat up dark red 1929 Ford Model A Roadster.

Jeremiah's betting parlor, whenever Gillie had the craving, occasionally sufficed. The local police turned a blind eye to the activities there, especially on this most auspicious of racing days. Besides, when off duty, most of the force frequented the parlor themselves. They were quite fond of Jeremiah, the big, burly black-as-tar Negro without a last name and a heart of golden kindness. Most of the time, he forgave their losses, wiped out their gambling debts – if they weren't too large and the take was good that night – and generally catered to their more prurient needs. No questions asked. In return, they allowed him to run his "establishment" without harassment; even bringing in more business by introducing Big J's to members of other police units in the area.

Gillie, himself, was a particular favorite of Jeremiah, although he was not a policeman. "Just a farmer" and a poor one at that. Yet, according to Jeremiah, there was something about the tall, lanky Irishman that reminded him of himself. So, he cut him a break whenever the chance presented itself.

That Saturday afternoon, when Gillie walked into the front of the saloon, he greeted Amos, the barkeep, with a nod and a tip of his dirty brown felt derby, and disappeared behind the double-doors that led into Big J's.

He quickly gave Jeremiah his $100.00 bet, half of his crap winnings. It, and the other half, was all the money he had left in the world, but he was doubly sure that Weston, a big two-year-old chestnut sired out of Madcap Princess by Sun Flag and trained by Jack Young, would win. Gillie had liked the description he had read in *The Daily Republican* that morning.

And he liked the odds, running at 40-1, even better. It was definitely a long shot, but his luck was holding and if he won, he would have $4,000.00.

More than enough to easily restore the farm to its former, pre-Depression glory.

But that was not to be.

Weston ran a decent race, but he finished dead last. Omaha, a favorite, claimed the roses. Gillie had lost his bet.

"There goes the new bull," he quipped, ripping up the betting chit into tiny shreds and tossing them into the sawdust on the floor.

Thinking his luck was running out and forgetting he had big plans for the farm – and for his wife and their expected son – he decided that the better use of the rest of his crap money would be to amble down to Abigail Hopper's. She'd be good for a lark and a romp, which would definitely take his mind off his troubles.

"Besides," he said out loud to no one in particular as he strode out of the sleazy tavern, once again tipping his hat in greeting to Amos, "she'd be all too happy to oblige me. As I would her."

He was chuckling all the way as he hiked up Nutt Road and then east on Bridge Street toward the Phoenix Hotel.

When his wife went into labor all alone, by herself in the early morning hours in the now shabby Victorian-styled master bedroom of the O'Rourke farmhouse and gave birth to their son, Flynn, Gillie was soundly asleep in Abby's arms.

Flynn inherited the farm in 1955 when he was barely twenty years of age. He had been too young to join the war effort; too old to be pampered any more by his mother. At twelve, his father had put him to work tending the chickens.

"Just about all he's good for," Gillie had said within earshot of his son, his only child. At least the only one he was aware of.

By the time Gillie had died of septicemia caused by a festering internal wound sustained when he fell dead drunk off the rusty tractor while plowing a field, the farm was more than run down. Only five aging, skinny cows were left. They barely produced enough milk to take care of Flynn and his ailing mother, let alone sell any to the local markets.

The barn roof was sagging; the large three-story house was badly in need of repair. A few bricks were chinking out of their mortar, falling onto the now weedy, overgrown grass, once Paddy's pride and joy. Many of the fields not used for pasture, normally planted each year with corn, barley, and a variety of seasonal vegetables, had been left to fallow. Only voluntaries grew. And they were sparse at best.

His mother had tried to do what she could, taking on most of the household chores herself – they had long ago not been able to keep any of the large staff her father-in-law had had when she'd first been wooed by the handsome gambler and had married into the family. But she was ailing herself and could not keep up with the tasks, especially the more arduous ones. Cursing her dead husband, she turned to her son for help

With the booming after-war economy and his own will-to-succeed attitude, young Flynn O'Rourke set about to make the wrongs his father had promulgated right.

In charge for all those years of the hen house and

now a gaggle of geese – he had grown an affinity for the Emden's while a young lad – the poultry business had flourished. With the egg business again turning a profit, Flynn had made enough money to feed himself and his mother and each week had some left over to save toward purchasing, again at a Kimberton auction like his grandfather, three young cows and a young steer. Unlike his great-grandfather father, though, he trucked all of them together in a large wood-slatted truck to the still intact Mingo farm.

In time, under Flynn's young, yet capable hands, the farm once again began to thrive. In a few short years, the young male bovine had fully grown into a handsome, active bull. The herd was back up to twenty cows, and then thirty, producing more milk than Kathleen, his new wife, and a newly-hired hand could process in a day. Sales increased at the new Forresta's general story, then at Redner's, and then at the small A&P off Nutt Road. Local residents clamored for the signature O'Rourke Dairy brown eggs produced by free-range hens, freshly churned butter, and various varieties of well-aged cheeses.

In the mid 1960s to early 1970s, when most of his fellow farming neighbors sold their land to reap the benefits of the burgeoning housing boom, Flynn was a hold-out, refusing to sell. Actually, like many of the others, he really didn't have to. He was doing quite well. Much better than he had ever imagined.

The land and the cows and the chickens and geese growing upon it – all that he had – were, in fact, profusely producing. O'Rourke's Dairy was making money. A lot of money. It was more than enough. So was the sizable investment account he had once started slowly, and was now more quickly building up; astutely managed by Jake Altmeyer, the smart investment counselor now employed by the Phoenixville Bank and Trust building on Main Street.

Now, on that morning of March 31, 1978, except for the loss of three of his prime geese early yesterday morning, Flynn O'Rourke was at the very top pinnacle of his game.

He thought he had cleaned up all of the dead geese feathers and carrion fragments the day before. But on his way to do the morning milking, he saw more. Frowning, he picked up a rake and began another sweep of the barnyard. He was worried that Kat might have seen any of it the morning before when she crossed to the processing room. If she had, she didn't say. In any case, he was determined to clean up every last fiddly bit before his prone-to-nervousness wife arrived to do that morning's milking chores.

He was busy working when he heard the putt-putt sound of a small engine. He watched as Kelly Pearce tooled up the long lane in her pristine low-slung yellow convertible and parked it just a few feet from the barnyard. Flynn rested the rake against the split rail fence and amusingly waited as the short, compact woman angled out of her car and sloshed through the drying mud.

"Ah, Mr. O'Rourke. I am glad you are here. I am Kelly Pearce..."

"Yes, I know who you are," he said, his gravelly voice echoing against the side of the red barn. "You here 'cause of my dead geese?"

"Well, it may be more than that," she stated. "I was at the Columbia last night and heard you and Mr. Reilly arguing...and, later, after you left, Billy Bushmill's account of...

"Billy Bushmill, huh?" O'Rourke asked, silently chuckling to himself. "He sometimes comes around during the winter, looking to sleep it off in my semi-warm hayloft in exchange for doing a few odd jobs around the place. I still keep an old horse blanket up there for him. Just in case, you know." He rubbed the back of his neck, well-tanned from years working in the fields. "Although, he hasn't been around for a while. How's he doing?"

"He came in after you left and claimed he saw the monster swimming up river from Pawlings Road."

"Uh. That so? Well, I, er, well. He is the most

honest man I know. Even if he is the town drunk..."

"Then his story is to be believed," Kelly said half to herself.

"Well, I don't know," O'Rourke smiled. He looked into the reporter's all too eager face. "Well, could be."

"Then...Well, in that case, if you don't mind, I do have a few questions." She took her steno pad and a pen from the messenger bag slung across her shoulder. "Do you mind if I take a few notes?" She clicked the Parker T-Ball jotter three times and began to write.

"Is all that, this necessary?" he asked, moving to open the barnyard gate to finally let her in. "I mean, a newspaper article....All that publicity. You know?"

"Might just be good for business," Kelly retorted. She was familiar with the grisly farmer's reputation for being a bit of a cagey wag, even if he was growing increasingly wealthy. "Free publicity and all, you know."

"Yeah, that might be true. But I'm selling enough, right now. Not sure if I could handle any more business. But your readers? Learning how my farm was, is maybe being invaded by a river monster, might scare my current customers away."

The last thing he wanted was his name in the paper connected with whatever it was that killed his geese. More important than losing customers, he still didn't want Kat to read or know about it. With her proclivity toward fearing the worst and the recurring nightmares, he was afraid she'd once more "go over the deep end". She had done that a few times in the last five years. He was determined not to let her go through it again.

Yet, with this persistent reporter, what choice did he have? He'd have to finally tell his wife the truth before the article was published.

"A river monster, Mr. O'Rourke? Why...?"

"As you said, you were there last night, Miss Pearce. You heard me...Reilly and I tell our tales."

"And Billy Bushmill, too. His description was quite detailed."

"Well, then. There you have it," the farmer smiled. "From the very mouth of Honest Billy. What else could it be?"

Kelly fairly danced with excitement, now hearing someone who was directly affected by the creature confirm what she thought she already knew. A real, live Lock Ness Monster here in Phoenixville. Right here in the very waters of her, their very own Schuylkill River.

"Well, I...Yes, I guess perhaps you are right. Could you tell me more?"

"I'll do even better than that, I'll even show you."

As he led her across the other side of the barnyard and down the path where he first saw the large groove carved in the mud, he thought about Kathleen and her seemingly irrational phobias. She was, by nature, a sensitive soul and a childhood trauma had made her even more so.

On a trip to Ireland with her parents as a child, Kathleen had been raped several times by her aunt's husband. Afraid to say or do anything, she was severely traumatized and had been suffering infrequent, but hallucinatory nightmares every since. She had explained the night he proposed to her that, set off by stress and fearful things, her dreams were so vivid, she would believe they were actual events in her life. She had gotten to the point that if something did frighten her, she would be afraid to go to sleep. There is no telling what will set an episode off again.

Flynn had promised that he would keep her safe, out of harm's way. He was now concerned that a story about a supposed monster crawling up out of the waters of the Schuylkill to kill their animals would bring Kat's nightmares back.

Yet, how could he avoid it?

"If it was a monster, as everyone is now saying it is," he explained to Kelly, indicating the large, smooth rut leading down the bank to the river, "it probably made this."

"Gad, how big do you think it is?"

"The groove looks to be about four, maybe five feet wide...If that's its main body, I think it would be maybe..." He paused to do a few mental calculations. "Ten or fifteen feet in length, Maybe longer. Wouldn't you say?"

"Including its neck and head."

"Neck?"

Kelly fished the manila folder out of her bag and showed him the picture of "Nessie", the Loch Ness Monster first sighted in a Scottish Highlands Lake on May 1, 1933.

"Barbie Altmeyer, the little girl who says she saw something in Lock 60, described what might be a miniature version of 'Nessie' here. It had a long neck, like the one a fisherman saw at Black Rock Dam and Billy, swimming under the bridge. Except she called it 'Skokie'. Do you think they all could be related?"

"I have no idea," Flynn smiled quizzically, talking off his faded green Eagles baseball cap to scratch the top of his head. "Could be, though. As I said, I didn't see it myself. Just the damage it, er, wrought." He put his cap back on and then flicked a few of the remaining scattered feathers alongside the groove away with his boot.

"It coincides with the descriptions I heard last

night...and what's on the police blotter...And what the description Jimmy Slaughter down at the waste plant gave to Sergeant Henderson. So, don't you think it could be, really was, is a river monster, Mr. Flynn? Like the one in Loch Ness?"

She was pressing him for a definitive answer. An answer, in all good conscience, that he, having second thoughts, couldn't – or wouldn't – give.

"I don't know, Miss Pearce..."

"Kelly."

"Alright, then, Kelly. I rightly, honestly don't know. Like I said, I didn't see anything, just heard it."

"But could you say something, er, um, definite as to what it was?" she pressed.

"No, but whatever it was...slithered right out of the water, invaded my rookery, killed and ate three of my prime, blue ribbon geese...And was large enough to slither back into the river, making this groove. If that is what you want to call a 'monster', like your Nessie, then," he hesitated before nodding, grinning shly, kicking more feathers away. "Um...then...well...so be it."

Kelly wrote down exactly what Flynn had said, stuffed her pad and pen into her bag, shook his hand as she profusely thanked him, then ran up the bank and across the barnyard to her car.

She had the crux of her story confirmed.

Now her remaining tasks before actually writing her article were to verify a few more of the actual sightings.

It was, she sighed as she drove down Township Line Road to its intersection with Route 23, going to be a long, but rewarding day.

She had failed to see O'Rourke grinning as she sped down the road, nor the large, wide-bodied Grumman canoe leaning against the broad side of the dairy barn.

"Thank goodness," he said to himself as he walked back through the barnyard to the rookery to tend to his prized geese.

"Had she seen it...Surely, the jig would have been up."

That night after supper, Flynn sat Kat and their daughter, Susan, down and, as gently as he could, told them, about their three geese and Reilly's mysteriously missing cow. Then he quietly told her about Sergeant Vicki Henderson's monster theory and Kelly Pearce's jumping-to-conclusions surmising about the various sightings by local residents of what they all were claiming to be a cousin of the Loch Ness monster in the Schuylkill River.

Susan cried over the death of Charles the First, then went out to the rookery to find another egg to hatch and raise. This one would be Charles the Second. Perhaps this young Emden pet would be luckier than her first.

After her daughter left, Kathleen continued to sit in the large drawing room. She hunched over, her head bowed, her hands tightly clasped between her knees, gasping for breath. She was numb and nervous at the same time.

She haltingly tried to explain to Flynn how more than upsetting it was to have not one, not two, but three seemingly inexplicable deaths on the farm in one day.

Especially the geese. Of all the animals they raised and cared for, they were the most like part of their family. And for them to be slaughtered by an unknown predator...It was unthinkable. What if it happened again?

"Who would do a thing like that?" she sobbed into her husband's shoulder. "Who?"

"More like a what," he whispered into her dark auburn curls. "More like a what."

"God help us," she snuffled. "God help us all."

It was going to be, for both her and her husband, yet another sleepless night.

TRACKING SKOKIE

By ten-thirty Friday morning, Kelly was back at her desk, cluttered with more phone messages about the monster she had by now fondly referred to as "Skokie", the name Barbie Altmeyer had shouted out from the barge yesterday afternoon.

Her "official" Map of Sightings and Incidences was laid out in front of her, now riddled with many lines drawn with yellow and blue highlights. Dates, times, and details of other sightings reported to her by Vicki and a few of the newspaper staff were scribbled in the blank spaces and in the wide border.

Thursday, 2:45. Hikers with their dog walking the Upper Schuylkill River Trail pass Black Rock Dam and see a "manatee" cavorting in the water as it swam upstream.

Kelly knew it was a fact that manatees could not have travelled this far north from Florida. While fresh water aquatic mammals – the Schuylkill was mostly fresh water with a hint of saline – they would have had to travel up along the Atlantic shore, navigating the briny waters. An anathema to their very health. They also preferred much warmer climes. Yet, she reasoned, Skokie did have a rotund body similar to that of the heavy-set, long, animal that roamed the Sunshine State's inter-coastal waterways.

Thursday, 4:30. A couple enjoying a pre-dinner cocktail river ride from the Spring City Pier to Black Rock Dam and back again claim "a small whale-like creature bumped the side of our Century Ski Boat, as if we were in its way."

Kelly was thankful the boat wasn't overturned. There were too many, often fatal, boating accidents in the waters above the dam. She had covered a number of them last summer and was loathe to have had to write yet one more tragic story along with the resulting obituaries.

Thursday, 6:30 p.m. Two teenagers walking hand-in-hand along the towpath a half mile above Fitzwater Station fearfully watch the canal waters suddenly start to roil and foam, as if being churned up in a Mixmaster. A large serpent, with a scaly head and large, round black eyes reared up out of the water...

"They must have been scared shitless," the reporter laughed. "Someone should have told you," she spoke out loud to them, "that unless you are fish or fowl, our Skokie is basically harmless."

As she plotted the monster's course, she saw that Nessie's cousin made headway up and down the Schuylkill, concentrating her wanderings in and around the upper portion of the canal by the lock.

"I wonder," she mused. "If that dang thing isn't thinking of nesting."

The Mysterious Expert

He had a wry grin, a sparse, pencil thin goatee and a long, drooping, a la Mark Twain sort of bushy mustache. Both were fading from black to grayish white. Intense black eyes, too small for his wrinkling, elongated face, peered out from under an old-fashioned wide-brimmed fedora. Dark brown felt, stained and bleached from one too many days working under the desert sun. His clothes, too, were from a much earlier era; quite unlike the crisply ironed chinos and colorful pants and tops that were de rigueur for the older residents who idled away their retirement afternoons in the Vale-Rio Diner.

He had been sitting in a back booth sipping weak Darjeeling tea – spiked with the dregs of whatever mysterious contents he clandestinely poured from his dented and tarnished hip flask – as he carefully listened to the locals jabber on about the news as reported in the previous day's edition of *The Evening Phoenix*.

What Validated Parking Needs: Leadership read one front page article published in the paper on March 30, 1978.

"Exactly what we need," Sam said, cozying up to

Celeste's counter. Without looking at one of menus poking out of a metal clip attached to the faux-granite marbleized surface, he ordered an open-faced turkey sandwich with "extra green beans, if you please". He turned to the other customers.

"With the influx of new people coming up from Philadelphia...invading our space, as it were...And with the new shops in town...there's no place to park. Charge everyone to park everywhere, that's what I say."

Lenny Leighton, still reeling from Casey's account of his seeing a monster in the river yesterday morning, scowled into his coffee.

"I pay enough taxes to live in this borough. Why should I have to pay more to park in it?"

"You don't have to," Sam countered. He, too, had been a native-born resident of Phoenixville. One of the older senior citizens who frequented the Vale-Rio, he had seen more than his fair share of changes in the area. The growth of the steel corporation, the demise of many businesses only to be replaced by new ones. The tearing down of the Phoenix Hotel, superseded first by a F.W. Woolworth's, then by a municipal parking lot which, by the way, had meters. Twenty-five cents for a quarter-hour.

"Your house on Third Avenue," Sam said to Lenny, "has a garage out back. You can walk anywhere in town."

"Not with my arthritis. Besides, with Leah now gone, the good Lord rest her soul, I may be just thinking of moving..."

"To Phoenixville Manor out on Main, huh? They don't allow residents to have cars there, so's you won't have to worry about parking," another customer jeered.

"Shut your trap," Lenny said to no one in particular, then stormed out the door.

"Just as well," Sam said. "He's getting more ornery by the day, now that dear Leah is gone."

"But he's right, you know," Celeste said, clearing away Lenny's half-empty coffee cup. "Parking is a problem in the borough. And will be for a long, long time to come."

After a lull, talk soon turned to the cutoff of water and sewer service to those in the area who hadn't paid their bills.

"How long they got?" Sam asked, slurping gravy from a tablespoon.

""Until April third," Kelly Pearce quipped, strolling through the door. After what she saw out at O'Rourke's Dairy, coupled with the photographs Mr. McGinty had given her that morning, she was getting a bit edgy.

What if the monster stuck again? And if it did,

where would that be? Where was it now?

Already that day, she had read earlier in the police blotter, a big lumbering black and white basset hound answering to the name of "Candy" had been reported missing from a backyard on Jacob's Street along the canal. Could that incident be related?

And there were a few other reports of other "Skokie" sightings up and down the branches of Schuylkill River that bordered Mingo.

She wondered if that was where Skokie lived. Had a nest? Slept at night?

Celeste laid a colorful paper placemat with puzzles and Disney Donald Duck cartoons suitable for coloring in front of Kelly as she settled herself in a booth just in front of the customer sporting the brown fedora and salt-and-pepper goatee.

"What'll it be, honey?" the waitress, cum part owner asked, taking a pencil stub and a small order pad from the pocket of her blue and white apron. "The usual?"

"No, Celeste. I think I'd like one of your famous Western Omelets with a double order of crispy French fries. I didn't have any breakfast and I am starving."

Celeste jotted the order down. As she wrote, Kelly noticed her gnarled fingers and the crimped wrinkles around her eyes and over her pursed lips.

She's getting old, the reporter sighed to herself. She's a legend in this town, fading fast. She was sure that when Celeste went, the Vale-Rio Diner would all too quickly become only a memory of a distant past Phoenixville that had, in the future, seen better days.

"And to drink?"

"Coffee, Please. Hot and sweet."

"Coming right up, hon."

When Celeste returned to the kitchen to turn in Kelly's order, Sam sashayed over to her table and asked about the monster.

"Any more sightings?"

"No, none today," she lied.

She wasn't about to say anything more about "Candy" being gone, lest the family be bothered by the more curious residents.

She knew the family, the Montoya's. With five children; all girls. One of the first Latino families to settle in Phoenixville. They were immigrants from Mexico. Legal, of course. Or so she had assumed. The oldest girl, Juanita, was already seventeen and desperate to be a newspaper reporter "like my friend, Senorita Kelly".

Juanita had stopped by the paper's offices one

afternoon after school, looking for back issues of *The Daily Republican*, the paper owned and published for many years by the Gilkyson family whose descendents now still lived in the big, yellow plantation-style house in Mont Clare.

"I am looking for articles about the German prisoners of war...World War Two," she had carefully explained. "They were garrisoned at what is now the Valley Forge Christian College."

"That is correct," Kelly had responded. "Why do you ask?"

"I am doing a project at school. My senior year thesis. Phoenixville schools – Momma Mia – getting so hard these days."

Kelly marveled at the young adult's persistence as she directed her to the Historical Society of the Phoenixville Area housed in the old Lutheran Church on Church Street.

"David Frees can help you there. There are back issues of the local paper on microfiche. And then I'd suggest you actually go to the college and see if someone in the Storms Research Center can't help you."

"And you? Can't you help me?"

"When you've done your research and are ready to write the paper...Yes, I can. I would be happy to help you."

With Kelly's guidance, Juanita had aced the paper and had graduated with high honors. She and the young woman's family had been friends ever since.

Remembering the day Mrs. Montoya had brought the plump puppy home from the local SPCA , Kelly was saddened by the loss of Candy, the now rather larger-than-life Basset hound who, she hoped and prayed, had not been taken by the monster in the river.

Celeste nudged Kelly when she placed the fluffy omelet in front of her.

"Daydreaming?"

"Just lost in thought."

The monster? You know my son, Billy, saw it. Under the Pawlings Road Bridge."

"Yes, I know. I was there yesterday when he came into the police station. And then again at the Columbia."

"Dead drunk, I presume."

"Yeah," Kelly grunted, digging into her first meal of the day. "But he's the most honest guy in town. So why won't I and Sergeant Henderson believe him?"

"I certainly do," the customer in the booth behind Kelly said. His voice was one tone above a lilting baritone. Oily, yet soothingly sweet. He spoke just above a whisper so that only Kelly and Celeste could hear. The aging waitress quickly nodded her exit with a warning lift of her right eyebrow, indicating that Kelly should be careful.

"And you are...?" Kelly sensed another part of her page one story in tomorrow's newspaper was about to unfold. She took out her well-worn steno pad and red T-Ball Jotter from her messenger bag. "I mean, your name."

"I'm from the University of Pennsylvania...the Department of Unexplained Phenomenon, don't you know," he said, his slim, almost gaunt frame towering over Kelly's short, prone to be slightly stocky one huddled in her booth behind a plate of scrambled eggs, ham, and green peppers.

"A local policewoman investigating the various, um, occurrences called me in to help with her case," he explained, thoughtfully stroking his short beard.

"May I?" he asked, indicating the other side of the table. Without waiting for Kelly's assent, he slid into the seat across from her, helping himself to one of her French fries.

Kelly didn't loose a beat. She was used to charlatans and this man sitting in front of her surely was the epitome of one. And one of the ruder ones, at that.

Along with his stealing her fries as he spoke, she

thought it equally rude he had not removed his dirty fedora. A little respect for my profession, and my gender, she thought to say. But then decided not to.

"Sorry, didn't catch your name."

"Later, my dear. Let's first talk about your, um, monster. You say you have evidence of sightings? Up and down the Schuylkill?"

"Yes, but how did you know?"

"I have my ways. Unexplained phenomenon, remember? Second sight and all that." He took another French fry and dipped it into the ramekin of ketchup Celeste had placed upon the table.

"Um, how about we get you your own order of these?" Kelly suggested, moving the plastic basket of potatoes closer to her plate.

"No, please. Don't bother. These are fine." He took another. "Now, about your so-called monster..."

"What about it...he...she" Kelly was now convinced it was a female, sheltering its eggs, its newborn just below O'Rourke's Dairy.

"I have been investigating reports of similar sightings in the Schuylkill in the coal regions and after the sergeant called and told me the story of the man who had been fishing illegally yesterday, I am guessing that the creature has moved downstream to habituate. Er, live. Raise its young."

Kelly nearly choked on a forkful of omelet. Her

shaky suspicions were proving to be true.

"That's what I thought, too."

"Well, my dear. You may want to jot this down for your article. I presume you are writing one?"

"Yes, for tomorrow's paper."

"The April First edition of *The Evening Phoenix*?" he smirked. "How utterly appropriate."

"How so?"

"If you don't know by now..." He munched thoughtfully on yet another fry. "Anyway...Here, write this down."

Kelly traded her fork for her pen.

"There is no question we must take this whole thing seriously," he continued. "Because we have documented information the creature is real. You may quote me on that."

Caught up in his supposedly valid account, Kelly told him about the photographs Charlie McGinty had given her. She was about to take them out of her bag, when she remembered she had left them in the manila file folder on her desk back at the newspaper offices.

"Yes, those, too...Although..."

"Although what?" she asked.

"The first thing you and the police have to do is assure the residents of this fair town that there is no danger to anyone. At least, not to people. My studies have shown that the river animal confines its diet to geese, chickens, and the occasional cow."

"That explains O'Rourke's loss," Kelly explained, furiously copying down the oddly-dressed stranger's words.

"Yes, those geese are really something," he said. "That serpent..."

"Is it really a serpent, with its flippers and all???"

"Oh, yes! Definitely. And it does have a penchant for geese. That is true. Personally, I prefer a good turkey, but the thing – she – really likes geese."

"Then, it's a she? For real?"

"Yes, really, a prime female example of the species. As I said, it has probably come downstream to spawn..."

"Then somewhere in the river, there had to be a male. For her to mate with? So she can lay eggs. Have babies?"

The strange man looked at Kelly quizzically, his hand poised in mid-air to grab yet another fry.

"Well, yes, I suppose, as you say, there must be. Another one. Huh. I hadn't thought about that. I always thought these creatures to be hermaphroditic. I never considered they'd be otherwise. But now that you mention it...That does make sense."

When he reached for another sliver of fried potato, Kelly finally got up the nerve to brush his hand away.

"That's enough. Get your own order," she sneered, waving for Celeste to come over to the booth.

"Another order of fries," she called across the aisle as the waitress approached. "For him."

"No, that's fine," he said, gesturing to shoo Celeste away. "I think I've had enough. And you've had enough...How shall I say it? Food for thought? Fodder for your article tomorrow?" He rose to go, tipping his hat to both Kelly and Celeste, who stood indignantly, fists on hips, in front of the counter.

"Um, don't you have any more comments about this monster who now swims up and down our section of the Schuylkill River like it was its own private swimming pool?" Kelly asked, pen once again poised over her pad."

"Sure. Here's my information." He placed a business card next to her plate, and then smiled. "This is all you'll need to know, to learn the truth about this story," he said, tapping the card for emphasis. "When you finally have enough sense to look at my name...and then look at a calendar."

Before Kelly had a chance to glance at the small, grey-tinted card with dark blue italicized lettering, he once again tipped his hat, winked knowingly at the reporter, leered a smarmy half grin at Celeste, and strolled confidently out the diner's door.

He crossed Nutt Road, weaving between cars and trucks, ambled up Bridge Street, and then slowly disappeared into the rain.

Whether his shoulders were shaking from laughter or the dismally chilly weather, Kelly couldn't tell.

"What a strange man," Kelly said, picking up the card. "I wonder…" She glanced briefly at it, curious about the choice of colors, but did not register what it said. When Celeste walked over to the booth to clear away the dishes and leave the check, she hastily stuffed it into the pocket of her leather jacket.

"Did you know him?" the waitress asked. "He seemed friendly enough…"

"I guess. But does it really matter?" Regardless, of who he was or what was on the card, Kelly knew she would incorporate all that he said into her article.

This was turning into a real coup of a scoop.

Nancy Crockett would be pleased.

Just wait until the residents of Phoenixville read her article in tomorrow evening's paper.

"He was certainly an odd duck," Kelly commented later that afternoon when she related to Vicki what the Professor of Unexplained Phenomenon told her at the Vale-Rio.

They were sipping hot, unsweetened chamomile tea out of Styrofoam cups in the common room of the police station where the officers on duty took their breaks and traded notes on tickets they'd given out, arrests they'd made, and the odd, rare cases they were working on. Outside of the occasional domestic squabble and out-of-towners speeding down Bridge Street, the more serious crimes rarely happened in Phoenixville.

"A duck, you say?" the sergeant quipped. "A fowl, like the geese and chickens he said the monster is so fond of eating? It's a wonder if he wouldn't be its next victim."

"He doesn't seem like the type to go near the water..." Kelly said seriously, not catching the joke.

"Oh, don't be so sure about that. So, did you get a chance to get his name?" Vicki, of course, was the "local policewoman" who had called the professor. She was eagerly anxious to see the look on her friend's face when she learned who he really was.

"He gave me a business card." Kelly fished into her jacket pocket, feeling around the used tissues, sticky Life-Savers, wads of paper, and loose change.

"Hey, Sergeant Vicki!" Chief Paderewski's voice boomed as he stoop-shouldered into the room and walked over to the make-shift kitchen area. "Here's someone you both will be happy to see." He bent down and beckoned. "Come on, girl. You look like you could use a drink," he said softly to the young two-tone basset hound that lumbered in behind him.

"Candy!" Kelly exclaimed. "Where have you been ol' girl? Your folks, especially Juanita, will be very glad to see you." She leaned over to scratch Candy behind her long lupine ears and came up with a handful of dried, caked blood. "What happened to you?"

Vicki drove Kelly and Candy in her squad car to Dr. Woldenhuff's animal hospital. "It won't hurt to get her checked out," the sergeant had said, calling Dr. W. on the police radio to alert him they were on their way.

The siren blared through town, alarming the residents who heard and saw it whiz up West Bridge Street to the veterinary. Despite having gone missing for two whole days and the obvious wounds on her neck and back, Candy wasn't the worse for wear. She stuck her nose out of the opened back window, sniffing the passing breezes; her short hind legs firmly perched on Kelly's thighs.

Emily McGinty greeted them in the reception area and then quickly walked the hound into an examining room where the gruff Dr. Woldenhuff was waiting.

Thirty minutes later, he and Emily reappeared with Candy in tow. A saddle patch of hair had been shaved from across her shoulders and there was a thin line of small stitches dotting up one leg and across the nape of her neck.

"She's a lucky dog," the vet said as he shook his head at the reporter and policewoman. "Had the good sense to walk into the police station like she did. Not that she would have bled to death...but I put in those stitches to close the wounds up. They'll heal quicker that way. I also gave her a tetanus shot, an antibiotic, and a rabies booster. Just it case."

Doc W., as he was fondly known in the community, was, despite his outward gruffness, a kindly, sometimes too overly cautious veterinarian.

"Do you think another dog, a bigger one got her?" Vicki asked, making a mental note to chide Candy's owners to keep a closer watch on their wandering basset.

"No. Those teeth marks – that's what they are – Don't seem to be canine. They're from a creature, much larger, I think. Maybe tried to pick her up and carry poor Candy away." He reached down to scratch her back, just above the base of her tail. "No, those marks were probably made by a large serpent...of some kind."

Vicki smirked as Kelly took out her notebook and began writing. "Serpent...large...tried to pick dog up..."

"Do you think it was 'our' monster," she asked

Vicki who couldn't help but smile."

"If it was, like your professor said, it certainly does not like the taste of hound."

FAIR REPORTING

The next morning, with a rough, handwritten draft in her messenger bag, Kelly descended the back outside staircase from her second-floor apartment, walked down the alley bordering Superior Beverage and then up South Main to enter Seacrist's through the front door.

She purchased a copy of *The New York Times*, curious about the escapades of her former co-workers, and then hastened across the street to the municipal parking lot where she was forced to park her cherished Karmen Ghia.

As a resident reporter supposedly "serving the community", she wasn't charged the usual $2.00 fee for overnight parking. But, still, it galled her that anyone would have to pay for parking anywhere in a community where residents paid steep taxes.

She drove cross-town to the Vale-Rio Diner where she took a seat at the far end of the counter.

Breakfast that morning would be tomato juice with lemon, decaf coffee, poached eggs on buttered toast with boysenberry jam, and a double-sized side of hash browns.

It was going to be yet anther long day as

Phoenixville's star reporter and she needed all the fortification she could get.

Halfway through her meal, Sergeant Henderson and Lieutenant Abrams walked into the diner and, after cordially greeting Celeste and ordering coffee to go, ambled over to Kelly and sat on either side of her. A reporter caught between two police bookends.

"You're not really writing and printing that article about the monster," Vicki said. "Are you?"

"Is that a question or a statement?" Kelly said, swallowing a hefty forkful of hash browns. She wasn't sure if her friend's uncharacteristically serious demeanor that morning was a threat or just an observation.

"Well, I...We, Abrams and I, no longer think, "she caught her grammatical error. "Er, I, we don't think it's such a good idea." She paused, and then quietly added, "After all."

"Why?" Kelly demanded indignantly. "It's not your call to make, Sergeant Henderson. Whether I write the article or not is my business. And the decision to publish it is Mrs. Crockett's."

"We're concerned about the residents of this fair town," Abrams interjected. "Reading about a monster in the depths of the Schuylkill that eats fowl and goes after pet dogs would really set them on edge."

"That is not my problem. I report the news, not

interpret it for my readers."

"Then think of their safety," Vicki said.

"Again, not my concern. But isn't that yours? Besides, the professor said," she quoted more pompously than she intended, "...the monster won't come after humans. Only geese." Seeing that she had sufficiently rebuffed her friend and her companion, Kelly turned back to her plate of vinegary eggs.

"Now, if you don't mind, I have a busy day ahead of me and I'd like to finish my breakfast in peace."

When the officers did not move, Kelly sighed in exasperation. "Alone."

"Sure," Vicki nodded, grabbing her coffee. "Be that way." She got up, and then beckoned to the lieutenant.

As they quickly left the diner, she turned to him and said, "I told you it wasn't a good idea."

"Yeah, I agree," Abrams nodded. "We never should have started all of this in the first place."

It took Kelly less than an hour to type up her handwritten draft from the night before. She took another thirty minutes to proofread the article before handing it over to Nancy.

It was nearly lunchtime, close to the deadline

when copy had to be in the hands of the linotype operators. The paper had to be "put to bed" by twelve-thirty, certainly no later than one o'clock to allow time for printing, bundling, and delivery. Phoenixville residents thoroughly enjoyed reading *The Evening Phoenix* after dinner and the evening of April 1, 1978 would not be, if Kelly could help it, an exception.

"This is really good, Kelly Pearce!" Nancy called from her office twenty minutes later; loud enough so that every reporter and copyboy in the newsroom could hear. Kelly beamed. Praise from their editor was rarely publically shared. She was certain she'd have her front page byline in that evening's edition.

Growing up, Kelly was always told by her humorless father to always be "careful what you wish for". That way, he explained, "you'll never be disappointed." So, for years, well into her adulthood, she never allowed herself to get her hopes up. She always downplayed her expectations; of herself and of others.

Why she had assumed Nancy Crockett, the aging editor, would give her a byline, especially after shouting out her compliment to the whole newspaper staff, would be a humiliating question she would ask herself for many months afterward.

For, in fact, her article did appear on the front

page with the double-decker headline

UNEXPLAINED EVENTS PUZZLE POLICE,

UNKNOWN THIEF STALKS SCHUYLKILL

But, after all her hard work the past two days, her name did not.

"It's good, really good," Nancy tried to persuade the more than just disappointed reporter now standing dejectedly in front of her desk, holding a limp copy of that day's issue in front of her. "A fine piece of reporting. But..."

"But if it is, why not give me the byline I deserve?" Kelly whispered, afraid to show her true feelings of anger. "Or don't I?"

"You certainly do, er, did, Kelly. But I was only thinking of your reputation in this community."

"What does that matter?"

"Think of it. Residents will realize that all of this was really some kind of hoax. And then they won't ever again take anything else you write in the future very seriously. You are too good a reporter for you, for us to let that happened."

Kelly appreciated the compliment and the editor caring about her good standing on the paper's staff as well as in the community. However, they didn't assuage her feelings.

"But it wasn't a hoax. Nancy. I got the police reports from Vicki, my friend at the station. Why would she lie to me? I checked my sources twice. Three times."

"Think about it, Kelly. Sergeant Henderson is famous for her wicked, yet quite dry sense of humor..." the editor tried very hard not to smile, but couldn't help herself. "And so am I," she said, barely out loud, to herself

"What about the photo? From Mr. McGinty?"

"Blurry at best. No real proof."

"But, Nancy...er, Mrs. Crockett...I talked to most of the people who claimed they actually saw..."

"I am not sure how she did it, but I bet if you check your friend's log of her police activity for the past few days, she had managed to get to everyone before you did."

"But Candy, the Basset hound...the teeth marks."

"Ah, yes. Candy. Well, Sean Conner did call the paper just a while ago. Apparently she had somehow escaped the Montoya's backyard and had wandered up to the Conner's backyard where their big setter is still on his long tether. Candy, being the friendly hound that she is, got too close. Curly might have gotten upset at the interloper and, well...You saw the result."

"But she wandered into the station..."

"Where Vicki took advantage of the situation. Were you there when she called Dr. Woldenhuff?"

"No, but..."

"I think, if you think about, she clued the kindly vet in on the ruse. He also does, you know, have a, um, wicked sense of humor."

Kelly was crestfallen. But when she looked deep into the middle-aged newspaperwoman's fading, yet still steely-blue eyes, she sensed Nancy Crockett was telling the truth.

"So, you knew about it all along? You were in on it, too?"

Nancy Crockett nodded, suppressing yet another smile.

"Yes, I was. Am. Even at my age, I still can't resist a good story. Nor pulling the wool over someone's eyes."

"Like mine?"

Nancy Crockett smiled again. This time a bit ruefully. She knew deep down inside she had hurt the feelings of one of her more talented, up-and-coming star reporters.

"But how," Kelly asked, "How could a whole town be in on it, too? How could I have fallen for...?"

"You often do take things a bit too seriously, Kelly. And in your zeal for yet another byline – your first hard-core news story on the front page – you failed to, um, see the clues and incorrectly put all the pieces of it together."

Kelly frowned.

"Wait, wait. How about the professor? The weird guy who spoke to me at the diner yesterday...from the University of Pennsylvania. He said it was all true."

"Didn't he say Vicki had, um, called him?"

""Yeah...She said she did, too. And, wait, he gave me his card."

"I suggest you take a look at it."

Kelly again fished into the pocket of her leather jacket. She pulled out the now crumbled light grey business card of the supposed "expert".

"Huh," she winced, reading the name above the title.

LIRPA LOOF

She concentrated on the name for a minute or so before the realization finally came.

"So..." Kelly winced when she realized the meaning of the name.

"And today's date, Kelly?"

Kelly glanced at the paper's masthead. When the reporter noted what day it was, she glanced at the editor, and then started to smile, rearranging – this time correctly – the puzzle pieces in her mind and finally realizing the truth.

She grinned broadly.

"Of course," Kelly said. "Of course...Then it is...?"

"Yes," Nancy smiled knowingly. "Yes, it is."

FACT OR FICTION?

It all ended on the evening of Saturday, April 1, 1978 when the so-called fake accounting of a Loch Ness-type monster swimming up and down the Schuylkill River in and around the Upper Providence and Phoenixville area really did appear on the front page of that day's edition of *The Evening Phoenix.*

Professor Lirpa Loof, a Professor of Unexplained Phenomenon from the University of Pennsylvania, was actually cited as the expert in the matter. But he was, by all accounts, never listed in the roster of instructors at the esteemed academic institution. When called, the then university president cordially and amusingly denied Professor Loof's existence.

"Sorry I can't be of more assistance," he told the inquiring reporter on the phone. "But perhaps someone at our Museum of Archaeology could help. We do have, I think, documented evidence of Nessie sightings..."

Whether three geese, a chicken, and a cow were really lost on March 30, 1978 remains a mystery. Even if the accounts were true, the thief had never been caught and while remnants of the slain fowl were discovered, neither hide nor hair of the missing cow was ever found.

Also open to suspicion were the supposed accounts of sightings of a smaller version of a cryptoid kelpielatus** plying the waters of the Schuylkill River around Black Rock Dam and Lock 60.

According to a number of Phoenixville residents back then still living in the area today, it was all simply a prank. A hoax perpetrated by two bored policepersons, an aging editor with "a weird sense of humor," and a small handful of residents who could never resist a good joke. All staged to get a too-serious, but well-liked reporter to "lighten up" and, perhaps, to tickle the funny bones of borough residents who also might be guilty of taking life a bit too seriously.

Yet, the question does remain why the paper would report on what was considered outlandish and false information. Especially on the front page, normally reserved for more serious – and factual – news. Why not put the article on the funny pages? Or were the editors and publishers at the time seeking to give the supposed hoax credence? Surely the local newspaper wouldn't print false accounts or purposefully perpetrate a deception.

Was the article, in fact, to be believed? Was it all, indeed, true?

As one attempted to accurately recount the

events that led up to the writing of the article, one had to also factor in the alleged sightings of the Loch Ness monster, first sighted and photographed 81 years ago. Since then, there have been claims of sightings of other river creatures of her in large lakes and rivers all around the world. The most recent was the early 2016 sighting of "Nessie" in the Thames River, London. Recorded on video by one Penn Plate from a railway bridge, it is the clearest indication that the so-called monsters are, in fact, real.

So, if one can assume that these aquatic animals in varying sizes do exist, and are even today spotted and even photographed in other exotic places, might not one also believe that there was – and maybe still is – one of them living in the Phoenixville waters of the Schuylkill River around Phoenixville?

The question will always remain whether the sightings that Thursday in 1978 were just a one day affair.

Did "Skokie" really disappear as mysteriously as she appeared? Never to be seen or heard of again?

Or is she still amongst us, plying up and down the Schuylkill waters?

Perhaps. Perhaps not.

But, then again...

**A wryly constructed Latin term designating phylum and genus of the mysterious, hidden, if not obscure species of mythical creatures.

Epilogue

Swimming at a fast clip upstream, she was oblivious to the small group of members of the Historical Society of the Phoenixville Area hiking up the Schuylkill River Trail after the outdoor lecture and tour of Lock 60.

It was late in the afternoon of a mild Saturday in mid-March 2016, and she was in somewhat of a hurry.

Thirty-eight years ago she had planted her first clutch of eggs into the nest she had built on the western shore of the canal and her biological clock was ticking again.

Perhaps for the last time.

This was the occasion to visit the one male of her kind that managed to survive in the shadowy waters just above Lindfield and then swim back downstream to build another nest along the murky depths of the restored canal. This one would be slightly further up river, far away from the prying eyes and cruel hands of the young human pranksters who had so many years ago discovered and, sadly, destroyed all of her eggs. Save one.

Still mourning her loss of the others, when the last remaining egg hatched, Skokie – for she had somehow understood the ranting and ravings of the young humanoid child on the barge on that day so long ago and had adopted the name – cupped her one remaining fledgling under a front flipper and fled downstream to the deeper, more clandestine waters of the Delaware River.

There, on the Jersey side, beneath the shadows of the RiverWinds Golf and Tennis Club, just below where the Schuylkill flowed into the large river, she had nursed her one remaining young. When he was old enough, and big enough, she had patted his head with a flipper and sent him on his way down the Delaware to, perhaps, haunt the more elegant waters of the Chesapeake Bay.

She did not wish to join him, preferring the shallower, more serene and less densely populated area in and around the prosperous Borough of Phoenixville. On the few occasions when she did allow herself to be seen, Skokie had observed that the residents were of the sort to see and not tell. Over the years they had proved to her that they were capable of minding their own business without meddling into hers.

And so, after launching "Schulk" on his long life's journey, she swam back up her river. It took the better part of two weeks, swimming underwater during the day so as not to be seen, avoiding the many pleasure boats and commercial ships. At night she stopped to rest and partook of the plentiful local fowl and fauna on both shores.

When she returned to Phoenixville proper, she decided it would be best to lay low for a while, paddling under the river's surface during sunlight, feasting on the large catfish that scavenged the bottom of the riverbed. At night she broke the surface, occasionally slithering upon a shore to eat local vegetation to replenish her stores of nitrogen and potassium.

She refrained, however, from slithering up the shore to O'Rourke's Dairy, now run by Susan, Flynn's daughter, who still raised Emden geese in honor and loving memory of her father. Skokie had, instead, acquired a preference for the wild fowl that frequented the new wildlife sanctuary along the eastern shore of the river.

It was, all in all, for Skokie, a good life.

If not also a lonely one.

So, that early evening in March of 2016, not seeing the hikers wend their way along the former towpath, now walking path, toward the Spring City Pier, she had purposely and proudly raised her upper body up out of the water.

Just as if the river was still her own private swimming hole.

Just as if she owned it.

Which, by virtue of the fact that she lived in the river without being sighted or caught for all these years, she did.

The local author was still elated from the largesse of recent sales of her latest book at the society's museum – as well as at the local family pharmacy. She had decided at the last minute to join her fellow members and take the Lock 60 tour.

It was an annual spring event and, being a retired – yet a still very active – senior citizen who had lived longer in Phoenixville than she had ever had in her own New York hometown, she was avidly interested in the area's history. Since the museum director had just last week introduced her to a tourist as "our writer", she was most anxious to becoming more actively involved in the historical society.

"Besides," she had rationalized out loud, "I might get an idea for another historical novel."

And so the author sauntered along the trail, trying to ignore the blister developing on the bottom of her left foot, attempting in vain to curtail the scampering of her stubborn-headed basset hound as he strained at the full length of his 30'-long Flexi-

Lead.

She was tired of constantly pulling him back to her side, yelling, "Stop it!" and "Heel!", much to her own embarrassment and his chagrin. She was thankful for the respite when an older gentleman had offered to walk FrankieBernard for a while.

"I used to go cubbing at the Pickering Hunt Club during the summer," he explained. "So they'd be ready for foxhunting in the fall," he explained. "A rambunctious basset hound, even an older one, is no different."

And so it was that the author found herself lagging behind the group, slowly walking up the path. Trying not to limp. Enjoying the scenery. Admiring the serene waters of the river as they coursed passed her, flowing gently over Black Rock Dam, into the canal basin below.

She was startled when the waters suddenly started churning.

She stopped.

She watched as a large grey-green scaled serpent's head perched upon a wide, elongated neck suddenly rose up from the now roiling waters of the Schuylkill River.

The head turned, like the lens of a larger-than-life periscope, swept over the two shores, and then turned toward the short, slightly plump woman standing stock still on the shore.

Watching me. Watching her.

Skokie's black eyes slowly blinked closed. Then, after three seconds, opened.

Then she winked at the hiker.

"Well, I'll be damned," the writer laughed. "So, the story...the article from over thirty years ago. It really...it really was true. You really do exist."

She smiled as Skokie slowly winked again. It was almost as if she understood and was in on the secret. The woman waved as if they were – or could be – a human-to-creature version of bosom buddies.

Skokie shook her head up and down, slowly closed, then opened her large, deeply black eyes again, and then continued her journey up the river to once again spawn and, once again, perpetrate her uniquely enigmatic species.

Maybe this time she'd be able to hatch and raise a full clutch compliment of four.

And, maybe, someday, humans would believe in their existence.

She was sure the person on the shore already did.

The author watched as the smaller-than-Nessie cryptoid kelpielatus swam further up the river and disappeared into the rising mists.

A thunder storm was coming. Its rumblings

already heard on the horizon. It was time to retrieve FrankieBernard – a descendant, by the way, of the Montoya's beloved Candy – and head home.

She was thankful Skokie did not have a taste for hounds. Otherwise this, their first meeting together would have been quite disastrous.

"I will have to come back and visit her again," she said out loud. "I wonder....won't this be, however, a great tale to tell?"

Musing to herself, she gathered her basset from the kindly gentleman, made her excuses to the rest of the group, and quickly jogged back down the path to the parking area to retrieve what was once her aunt's beloved yellow Karmen Ghia.

She quickly ushered FrankieBernard into the front passenger seat of the newly restored classic car and drove a bit too fast up the lane parallel to Lock 60's canal to the park's entrance abutting the Mont Clare Bridge.

She was anxious to get home and begin writing the story.

References

Anonymous – "The Loch Schuylkill Monster", *The Evening Phoenix Centennial Edition*, Monday, October 3, 1988. Phoenixville, PA.

Anonymous – "Unexplained Events Puzzle Police, Unknown Thief Stalks Schuylkill", *The Evening Phoenix*, VOL. 89, No. 153, Saturday, April 1, 1978, Phoenixville, PA.

Marshall, Susan C. – "Some Irish Men Who Made Their Mark in Phoenixville", *The Historical Society of the Phoenixville Area Newsletter*, Mar 2016, Volume 39, Number 2. Phoenixville, PA.

Martino, Vincent, Jr. – *Images of America: Phoenixville*, ©2002 Arcadia Publishing, Charleston, South Carolina

Martino, Vincent, Jr. – *Then and Now: Phoenixville, ©2005* Arcadia Publishing, Charleston, South Carolina.

Seiscio, Adele Bane – "The Irish: Unsung Heroes of the Canal and Railroad Era", *The Historical Society of the Phoenixville Area Newsletter*, Mar 2016, Volume 39, Number 2. Phoenixville, PA.

Various Articles – *The Evening Phoenix*, VOL 89, No. 151, Thursday, March 30, 1978, Phoenixville, PA.

www.Wikipedia.org/wiki/Phoenixville_Pennsylvania

About the Author

An accomplished author, literary critic, and long-time resident of Phoenixville, June J. McInerney occasionally purveys the "unusual and inexplicable phenomenon". She humbly admits to being an ardent fan of both Nessie and Skokie.

Written tongue-in-cheek, *the Schuylkill Monster* is her first work of documentary fiction and is her third novel and the second in her "A Novel of Phoenixville..." series.

June's previous novels, *Forty-Thirty* and *The Prisoner's Portrait: A Novel of Phoenixville During World War II*, are receiving a modicum of 5-star review acclaim. Her collections of short stories include *The Adventures of Oriegh Ogglefont, The Basset Chronicles,* and *Cats of Nine Tales*. June has also written and published two volumes of poetry, and wrote the books and lyrics for four musicals that have been produced by various theater groups across the country.

When not writing, she walks with her beloved FrankieBernard along, among other places, the Schuylkill River Trail in the hopes of, once again, meeting Skokie.

And, like many other residents of Phoenixville, she immensely enjoys hearing – and telling – the occasional good joke.

Please visit June's Literary Blog at
www.JuneJMcInerney.com

Made in the USA
Middletown, DE
04 June 2016